"We Have Less Than Two Months To Find That Codicil. Or…We Could Always…"

Ally swallowed thickly as Finn let that suggestion hang, his eyes focused on her lips. She couldn't stop her plummeting heart every time he mentioned that codicil. It just reinforced the cold, hard truth of his return.

"So I don't have a say in this?" she asked softly.

A bare hint of surprise and irritation sparked in his green eyes. "I'm just trying to handle this situation as quickly as I can."

The bittersweet emotion sent a pang through her chest, making it hard to breathe. She'd have to deal with his leaving eventually, but memories of this time—their time—would sustain her through the lonely months and years ahead.

Because there was no way she'd settle for second best. If she couldn't have this man she didn't want any other.

Dear Reader,

Long before Princess Mary met Frederik, I started writing Finn and Ally's story. It was to be my fourth full-length novel, the most emotional one I'd written, and, as fate would have it, the first book that sold. Of course, Finn and Ally started out with different names, different jobs. Even different nationalities. Thankfully, they knew who *they* were supposed to be and put me straight!

I love a good lovers-reunited, forced-proximity story. There's something instantly intimate about rekindling passion, about revisiting an old flame that hasn't completely burnt out, despite a tumultuous past. If you could wipe that past and start all over again with someone, who would you chose?

I hope you enjoy reading my first published story, set in Sydney, my favorite city in the world. I know I'm absolutely delighted to share it all with you! If you're interested in reading more about how this book came to be, visit me on the Web at www.paularoe.com.

Love,

Paula

PAULA ROE

FORGOTTEN MARRIAGE

Published by Silhouette Books

America's Publisher of Contemporary Romance

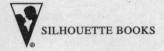 SILHOUETTE BOOKS

ISBN-13: 978-0-373-76824-0
ISBN-10:   0-373-76824-9

FORGOTTEN MARRIAGE

Copyright © 2007 by Paula Roe

Visit Silhouette Books at www.eHarlequin.com

Printed in U.S.A.

PAULA ROE

Despite wanting to be a vet, a choreographer, a hair-dresser, a card shark and an interior designer (though not all at once!) Paula ended up as a personal assistant, office manager and software trainer for thirteen years. Those years of filing systems, memos and interoffice email policies funded her backpacking trip through Europe, partying in Bali and sightseeing in North America. Then there's also the nine fun years teaching aerobic classes, complete with leotards and groovy dance music.... Despite life's distractions, she's never given up on her lifelong dream of becoming a published author.

Today, with western Sydney's glorious Blue Mountains as a backdrop, Paula lives with her family and an ancient black cat who can't be bothered chasing the rainbow lorikeets and magpies that frequent their yard. You can e-mail her at paula@paularoe.com.

To all the contest judges (especially Bronwyn Jameson, Robyn Donald, Trish Morey and Suzanne Cox) who read Ally and Finn's story over the years—my deepest thanks for every word of feedback. To Kerri, a gorgeous soul who always believed I could do it. To Karen, the best Dane I know. And of course, to Cooper—thanks, sweetpea, for letting mommy work as a full-time writer!

One

Married.

Finn Sørensen had a wife. And apparently she was living in Australia.

What a god-awful mess.

Finn swirled the untouched bourbon and ice around in his glass, ignoring the flight attendant's flirtatious smile as she walked down the darkened isle.

This mystery wife had also inherited a ten percent controlling share of his father Nikolai's jewelry empire. That is, if he found the missing codicil. If not, Danish law decreed the controlling share go to his father's current wife.

Marlene, his selfish, image-obsessed, cold-hearted stepmother who'd hold on to those shares from beyond the grave if she could.

Focusing his attention out the window of the first-class

section, he glared into pitch blackness, sixty thousand feet above the earth.

His life had been one surreal revelation after another since that December car crash had put his father in intensive care and wiped out much of Finn's memory.

From various photos and letters, he'd uncovered scant details—he'd met his wife last year in Sydney, Australia. Love at first sight, his cousin Louisa had recalled, starry-eyed.

And for every glowing avowal of love, his stepmother had produced the flipside. *Gold digger. Poor Irish immigrant. Secretive, sullen, argumentative.*

His mouth thinned. Marlene's educated lilt had been heavy on the insults and light on the details. Yet when he'd called her on it, she refused to elaborate.

"She ran out on you, Finn. You've never dwelt on the past, so forget about her and focus on the company."

How could he focus when he couldn't remember?

That damned tingling, like ants crawling over his skin, started up at the base of his spine. The undeniable sensation of half truths chewed and gnawed until a thin sheen of sweat broke out on his brow.

He swiped it away and took a shuddering breath. Marlene had been civil enough…up until the day his father had died. Then she'd stuck her claws right in, undermining his ability to run the company, swaying many of the board to vote her way. Now she was demanding an immediate settlement of his father's estate. His visit to the head office in Copenhagen had only produced more questions. Despite Nikolai's deathbed confession of a codicil, he was still missing any hard evidence. The company lawyers had no record of it, nor was there anything in Nikolai's private papers. And Finn couldn't remember.

He knew one thing—doing nothing meant he'd lose the

Sørensen legacy, his father's entire reason for living and breathing.

So he'd put his case to a sympathetic judge and received a two-month stay on the execution. And now he was chasing a long shot, flying twenty-six hours from Copenhagen to Sydney in hopes of triggering his memory and uncovering the truth.

Marlene's deceit continued to burn in his gut like a newly stoked flame. Until he knew more, until he could trust Ally— *if* he could—he'd keep the details of his father's bequest to himself. And when he *did* find that codicil, he'd offer her a good price. A win-win situation.

Yet, his conscience niggled, he must have trusted her once—he'd proposed. She had accepted. There must have been something between them…

Or Marlene could be right.

There was only one way to find out. Finn pressed a hand to his temple, rubbed at the throb that was slowing building momentum behind his eyes and whispered, "*For helve,* Father, what on earth were you thinking?"

The phone.

The soft trill broke through Ally McKnight's foggy but promising dream, and with a groan she groped. After knocking over a book, a bag of M&M's and a notepad on the nightstand, she finally found the receiver.

"For the last time, Tony, it's late," she muttered, keeping her eyes firmly shut as she snuggled back under the sheets. "I've been working all night and I don't need you checking up on me every hour just because I'm—"

"Ally?"

"What?"

"It's Finn."

Shock hit her like an off-course meteorite; her eyes sprang

open. Her breath gurgled in her throat and in the wake of stunned silence that followed, a dozen snappy comebacks teetered on her lips: "Who? Oh, right. The husband who didn't want our baby." Even, "Sorry, wrong number." All delivered with consummate cool that would have made an Antarctic wind feel tropical. Instead…

"Call me back at a decent hour!" she choked out, then slammed the receiver down with a shaking hand.

She was still glaring at the phone when it rang again.

"I've just charged my cell phone and I've got a pocket full of change," Finn said, unfazed by her rudeness. "I can keep calling all night."

"What do you want?"

"I need to see you." The deeply masculine voice, all warmth and sensual Scandinavian accent, sent a dozen unwelcome sensations shooting across her skin.

"Excuse me?"

"I need to—"

"See me, right."

What had happened to that touch of blasé she had perfected just in case this exact moment ever arrived? But now hell *had* frozen over and she sounded as nervous and awkward as a teenager.

She kicked off the sheets and stood. He was finally going to do it. Two months, three weeks and five days after she'd walked out on him, her husband had decided to sign those divorce papers and get rid of her for good.

"Ally? Are you still there?"

"Yes."

She waited. The silence just stretched loud and long until her curiosity threatened to snap. Finally she said, "Why?"

"I need a favor."

"A favor? What kind of favor?"

"For starters I'm stuck at the airport because of the transport strike."

"You're here? In Sydney?"

"Ja."

Ally sat heavily on the bed, the mattress protesting beneath her weight, and resisted the temptation to hang up again. "Why are you here?" she demanded.

"Look, Ally, I'm jetlagged and need a shower. Pick me up and we can argue about it then."

It was a typical Finn reply—a command tempered with that underlying "why are you being so difficult?" subtext. Yet the warmth, the sheer intimacy of his deep melodic voice invaded her common sense, stuck a knife into her heart and gave a vicious twist. And that traitorous mind of hers flashed back to Copenhagen International Airport.

It had been a cold December morning, the weather matching her mood—overcast, drizzling, gray. She'd been so naive, so in love. How quickly it had turned into heartbreak. So she'd left. *And now, after all that pain, you've finally shoved those memories into the past where they belong and he's back on your doorstep.*

"We're over," she said, anger dashing away the memories. "You said—" she nearly choked on her words, but pride refused to let her do it "—you're with someone else. What makes you think I'm interested in anything you have to say?"

The line went silent. Outside her bedroom window a dog barked, followed by the screech of car tires. Her quickened breath echoed down the receiver, a harsh reality in her ear.

Finally Finn said, "I thought we left our relationship as friends—"

"Friends don't fly across the world without giving each other notice." *And friends don't rip each others' hearts out,* she added silently. "We're not friends anymore, Finn. We're ex-husband and ex-wife."

"But we're not exes yet, no?"

Ally sucked in a breath, held it until dizziness forced her to exhale.

"Look," Finn said cautiously, "I understand—"

"You've never understood me. Just one of our many differences you liked to point out."

"I've got your divorce papers," he said tightly. "You need them signed, yes?"

"I can file them without your signature." She rubbed her eyes, still gritty with sleep.

Was that an aggrieved sigh she heard? Sure it was. He was comfortable with predictability and she frustrated the hell out of him because she was exactly the opposite.

"Dammit, Ally, why do you leave me no choice? Your apartment—"

"What about it?"

"I own the whole block."

Disbelief shot her to her feet. "How—? What are you playing at?"

"I don't play, Ally. Meet me and I'll tell you what I want. The florist downstairs. I'll be waiting."

The dial tone buzzed in her ear. *I don't believe it.* He'd hung up on her!

Son of a...

She slammed the phone back in its cradle so hard she thought she heard a crack.

He was joking. He must be. Damn him.

Clenching her hands by her sides, she forced herself to take a calming breath. Slowly, slowly, as she absently rubbed her barely noticeable twelve-weeks bump, their last argument reverberated in her mind like the bells of doom.

You never stay with one thing long enough, he had thrown in her face with all the fury and frustration written in his eyes. *You can't commit. Especially to our marriage. What kind of mother will you be?*

Did he want her back? She shook her head. Not this side of a millennium, not after what they'd done to each other.

Had he found out about the baby?

Panic kicked her heart into double time. He'd given no indication he knew.

What if she ignored him?

Bad move. He'd only take that as a challenge, turn on the charm and seduce her into agreeing with whatever he wanted.

That was how they'd ended up in bed. And married. She was a goner when it came to Finn. Persuasion—like his European good looks—were as natural as his devil-green eyes.

Ignoring her comfy slippers at the bottom of the bed, she walked into the bathroom, welcoming the cold chill of tiles beneath her toes.

Whatever he wanted, it was not a baby. He'd made it perfectly clear that his father's business took center stage.

Her face flushed bush-fire hot. Expected her to be unreasonable, did he? Well, he was in for a shock. She'd be the adult if it killed her. She'd hear him out, get those divorce papers back and leave. He'd be out of her life quickly, before he discovered how completely it had backflipped. Simple.

It would be one of life's little tests, as Gran was so fond of saying. No hysterics, no recriminations—despite those frustrating hormones racing around her body. Cool and calm. She could certainly handle it because all those old feelings were dead and buried.

She scowled at her reflection in the mirror, her features distorted by shadows and moonlight from the frosted window behind her. Of course they were over. There was nothing left except memories.

With doubts filling every dark and comforting space, she clicked on the light. The shadows fled like a cat caught in the headlights.

She dressed quickly in a pair of jeans and a long T-shirt, fussed with her hair and hid the faint circles under her eyes with concealer, all while her imagination clicked into overdrive.

The intense lovemaking, the urgent and consuming passion was a living, breathing memory, seared into her subconscious. He had stolen her heart in less than a month, left a lasting impression that no amount of willpower could erase. She'd never believed in love at first sight until Finn.

And she never would again.

Had his world shattered as completely as hers when she'd left?

Doubtful, she thought savagely. *He's not the one pregnant and unemployed.*

After padding down the hall to the living room, she yanked on her shoes then grabbed her keys from the hall stand.

As she locked her apartment then walked down the stairs to the car park, their naive promise when they'd met burned in the back of her mind. *No matter what happens, no matter who we're with, we should always remain friends.*

Friends. What a joke. Lovers can never, ever go back to being friends. Their history always ruins it.

For the sake of her sanity she tried not to think about how his body had felt naked, lying next to hers. How his kisses had made her weak with wanting. How just one look, one touch, was all it took and they were ripping their clothes off in a sexual frenzy.

Ally unlocked her car, got in, then gunned the engine. She'd do well to remember that sex could only go so far in a marriage—not like trust, commitment. Compatibility based on mutual likes.

There was a logical explanation for his appearance. Despite his breathtaking arrogance that was as natural as his polished social skills, Finn didn't possess one illogical bone in his body. It was March, a good time to be in Sydney for the tail end of summer, cheap flights from Europe…

Oh no. She slammed on the brakes and the car screeched to a stop on the bitumen. What if he wasn't alone?

She winced as she pictured some leggy, blonde Dane called Helena hanging off Finn's arm. Maybe they needed a ride somewhere. *Don't worry, darling,* Finn would have assured her. *She did say we should remain friends.*

The scenario churned around in her head until a car horn startled her. Easing her foot off the brake, she drove down the street and took the next turn left.

Well, Grandma Lexie had encouraged her to stand up to those curve balls in life. And now it was throwing a gigantic one by the name of Finn Sørensen.

Ally parked her small Suzuki in the international terminal car park, got out and strode toward the arrivals lounge. The cool night goose-bumped her bare arms, the car keys jangling in her nervous fingers. As she neared the large glass doors, trepidation slowed her stride to a walk.

Dread set in, tripping up her spine to lodge in her neck muscles. The doors swished open to allow her entry then silently closed behind. The terminal's distinctive smell enveloped her: plane fuel, coffee and new luggage.

She turned right, scanning the crowded arrivals hall. On a normal night the stores and cafés should have been closed but the strike had prompted some to stay open in an attempt to make a quick dollar. The coffee shop was doing a brisk trade, the newsstand had a line forming at the cash register. Only the florist remained shut.

And there he stood—alone—his long frame leaning comfortably against a wall, head buried in a newspaper.

Ally stopped fifty feet from her past, her stomach swirling with a thousand butterflies, and let the emotion wash over her. It was like a physical touch, tripping warm fingers of remembrance over her skin, leaving her short of breath and sweaty. Emptiness ached like a gaping hole in her chest for one brief second then was gone. In its wake, memories sent her body into its own little hum.

The warmth of his arms wrapped around her, the gentle, erotic rasp of stubble from his chin as it brushed against her cheek.

She glanced at the airport clock above and realized the hands had stuck at eight o'clock.

Almost as if time stood still.

Once, an eternity ago now, she'd wished desperately for that to be true. Because at the precise moment she'd dragged herself onto a Sydney-bound plane, their future together was gone. Throughout those endless hours in the air, she'd sat alone and silently cried for the home they would never make, the family they would never have, for her pride and the naive expectations that had shaped her decisions.

And it was all encapsulated into one clichéd greeting card moment in a cold, busy airport.

She suppressed a shiver and hardened her heart.

Despite the short hair that barely touched his collar and a slight paleness to his skin, Finn hadn't changed one bit. Those high cheekbones were as sharp as she remembered, his square jaw still with that kissable cleft dusted in stubble. All his features—some attractive, like his long-lashed emerald eyes, some downright out of place, like the noble nose with its broken bridge—were mishmashed to make a perfect package. He readjusted his body against the wall and Ally smiled humorlessly. Even after a long flight, Finn still appeared the epitome of cool in conservative jeans and sweater. Style was in his blood.

Yet… There was something disconnected about the way he stood there, about the way people passed by and he completely ignored them. He was a people person, thrived on the interaction and connection to other human beings. Now he seemed almost…lonely.

As she studied the man who was now a stranger to her, she continued to frown.

With an efficient flick he folded the paper, tucked it under his arm then casually scanned the area.

Like a sharpshooter zeroing in on his target, his green gaze locked on to hers. And the force and intensity of the past welled up inside, terrifying her. Lust and longing. Frustration of a thousand different arguments long gone. Shattered dreams.

And anger.

She let the heat of that last emotion burn with welcome relief, taking comfort in it. It was a far more polarizing emotion than the sudden heat of arousal that had blanked her mind of all rational thought.

She took a firm step forward, then another, until she was finally standing in front of him.

"If you've come all this way to tell me you're kicking me out…"

"And *goddag* to you, too, Ally. I'm not kicking you out."

The short reprisal combined with that curt admission brought her breath in sharply. "So it was just a ruse to get me here?"

"It worked, yes?" he said softly, his richly accented tongue wrapping around the syllables almost tenderly.

She clenched her teeth. "I should just leave you here."

"Don't." His hand shot out, gripping her arm. His touch electrified her skin, shocking her. She opened her mouth to snap out a demand, but he stymied her with his withdrawal and, "Thank you for coming out so late."

Confused but unsure why, she glanced around the crowded arrival hall. "No cameras or bodyguards for the vice president of Sørensen Silver? Makes a change."

"The press think I'm in Sweden taking a break. And the bodyguards only attract more attention. Here I'm just another tourist."

He swept his eyes down her body appraisingly, as if cataloging the changes since their parting. She nearly put a protective hand over her stomach but stopped herself just in time.

Not trusting herself to speak, she remained silent as his eyes continued to study her like a thousand trained spies.

She shifted her weight from one foot to the other. Adult Ally wanted to give him a controlled smile and coolly tell him she wasn't interested in anything he had to say. The other Ally—impulsive Ally—who'd trusted so easily and fallen even more easily in love, wanted to smack him in the eye for all the pain and hurt he'd made her go through alone. And then throw her arms around him and never let go. *But you did.* She reminded herself. *You did let him go.*

His familiar woodsy aftershave tapped against her hard shell of protectiveness, begging entry.

Cool or crazy, both ideas were stupid. Instead she said the first thing that came to mind. "Traveling light?" She nodded to his luggage trolley.

"*Ja.*"

That's a good thing, right? So he's not staying long. A trickle of nervous sweat beaded down her back, sticky warmth heating her armpits as she reached for the trolley. "Well, let's go. Where are you staying?"

"The Crowne Plaza at Coogee Beach. Ally," his hand tentatively covered hers, sending an intimate warmth buzzing up her arm. The small gasp welled up in her throat, but she choked it back down. He was so close she could feel his chest brushing her shoulder, the familiar intense heat of his body scorching into hers. So close she could reach out, trail her fingers down his cheek and savor the welcome graze of his five-o'clock shadow.

"What?" She swept her eyes downward, away from that too-inquisitive scrutiny.

"Thank you. I—"

Ally snatched her hand away. "You traveling alone?"

"Ja."

"So what's this favor you want?"

He frowned, cupped his cheek in his palm and rubbed. The familiar gentle rasp of stubble against skin sent screaming memories flitting across her subconscious, sending the butterflies in her stomach into a crazy dance. His I'll-take-what-I-want-because-I'm-so-charming arrogance had disappeared. In its place was something akin to uncertainty. The lines around his eyes denoted weariness, as if extreme sadness had personally etched out every one.

Confused, she found herself staring. Finn never bottled up stress, never agonized over past mistakes. He dealt with it and moved on. Whatever was eating at him must be serious.

Compassion flooded in, prompting her to gently touch his arm.

"What's wrong?"

Weary eyes met hers, so full of confusion and pain that she felt as if she'd been hit by the four-fifteen to Bondi Beach. She swallowed. Maybe she didn't want to know.

A second later, the look was gone and Finn's expression eased back into the familiar, in-control one.

"Let's get out of here."

Knowing she wasn't going to get any answers until he felt like giving them, she nodded and led the way out.

Driving in loaded silence, they pulled into the hotel car park fifteen minutes later.

Check-in was a blur, as were the smiles of the desk clerk, the offer to carry Finn's luggage and the elevator ride up to the presidential suite.

The elevator slid open to reveal a plush hallway with a door at either end. Finn turned left, leading the way as if he'd been occupying five-star hotels all his life.

And that, Ally realized as he carded the door and stepped aside to let her enter first, *is just another of our many differences.* With a gloomy cloud now over her thoughts, she took in the opulent suite in subtle gold and beige furnishings, the spacious lounge area that was bigger than her entire apartment. During the drive, her anger had been put on the back burner as nervousness of the unknown swiftly rushed in to fill the void.

She kept replaying that look on Finn's face. The sorrow. The hurt. The bare emotion so rarely displayed outside the bedroom. And it twisted her up inside wondering what—or who?—had put it there.

He sank into a plush lounge chair with a relieved sigh. "I forgot how long it took to fly to Sydney. How do you stand twenty-six hours in a cramped cabin?"

"I don't."

Ally placed her keys on the mahogany writing desk and glanced around the room with more calm then she felt. Ignoring his thoughtful gaze, she went over to the French shutters. Sweeping them open, she then unlocked the sliding glass door that led onto a private balcony and let the salt-and-ocean breeze sweep in. It lifted the hair off her neck, sending the shorter curls across her cheeks. She shoved them back, took a deep breath and exhaled, feeling the tension in her body ease a fraction.

"Do you want coffee?" he said from the couch.

She smiled thinly and turned. *Ever the gracious host.* "Then you'll tell me what you want?"

He nodded shortly.

"Fine. Tea, please."

It was a shock to the system watching Finn play the hired help—plugging in the dripolator, tearing open the ground beans packet and dumping it in the filter. By the time he laid out the sterling tea service on the antique coffee table and finally turned to give her his undivided attention, nauseous anticipation had seeped in. As she felt his eyes run over every inch of her body as though he'd not seen her in a lifetime, her resolve was slowly going into meltdown.

She nervously tucked a heavy lock of hair behind her ear—which only conjured unbidden memories of Finn doing the exact same intimate task. She quickly dropped her hand and sat on the couch arm as Finn brought the tea service to the coffee table.

"Don't tell me you came all this way to hand-deliver those divorce papers," she said at length.

He crossed his arms, bands of muscle tightening across his chest. She met his eyes, half expecting the cold, hard cynicism reflecting in the green depths. But he just walked silently past her to the balcony door, giving her his back. She let her gaze drag down his long body as he stared out into the dark star-speckled night. The broad shoulders, the trim waist. The fabulous backside that always set off a pair of jeans to perfection…

"No. But they shocked the hell out of me."

Ally shook her fuzzy head. *Focus. The divorce papers.* She put the sugar bowl on the tray with a thunk. "Why? We were over. I was never good enough for your family, for the

Sørensen's blue-blood son." She poured a dash of milk in her cup. "I had no money, no breeding and no class. I left and you moved up to the vice presidency. Coincidence? No." She glanced up just in time to see him turn and shoot her a puzzled look before she focused on the herbal tea box. "How does your new girlfriend feel about this little visit?"

"Jeanette left while I was in hospital."

In the claustrophobic silence that followed, Ally thought he was waiting for her to say something, to offer condolences. She refused. Vocalizing false comforts would make her a liar and she wasn't about to start doing that.

Hang on. Hospital?

As if reading her mind, he said, "My father and I were in a car crash. He died last month."

Her spoon clattered on the saucer. "Oh, Finn, I'm so sorry. I didn't know…" *Of course you didn't.* She paused and stood, feeling uncomfortably inadequate, before blinking away tears. "When? How?"

"Before Christmas. A drunk driver. My father was in the passenger seat."

Worry thumped her heart double-time. "You're okay, aren't you? Were you hurt?"

"I cracked a few ribs, got a concussion. Nothing permanent except…" He tapped his head.

"Brain damage?"

He smiled thinly. "An infection put me in a coma for a week. It wiped out a lot of my memory."

"Your—? Amnesia?" Ally stared, her eyes rounding. "So you blocked out the accident?"

He nodded grimly, that one gesture revealing a sea of frustration behind it as shadows twisted his expression again. It was starting to get to her. It made her itch to smooth away the lines of worry. To hold him. Comfort him.

"I can read and write, all the basics. And after rehab a lot more returned. But the last few years are still one big blur."

He paused, waiting for her to join the dots. Ally knew her mouth hung open, her look one of frank disbelief, because it clearly reflected in his eyes. Before she had a chance to assimilate that revelation, Finn spoke again.

"I've been trying to remember but I come up blank every time."

Ally jumped as he closed the distance between them in a blink. When he placed his hands on her shoulders, his touch seared through her thin shirt, branding her with familiar aching heat.

"I've been reading your old letters and I…" He paused, took a jagged breath. "I spent hours trying to find a trigger to unlock my memory. There was nothing except those damned divorce papers."

Ally could only stare at him as her heart hammered in her throat. Shock, disbelief and dread all mingled in the pit of her stomach, threatening to rise up and choke her. He didn't want her back. He didn't know about the baby. He wanted… What *did* he want?

His green eyes, complicated windows of bundled emotion, bored into hers. "I need answers. I need *you* to help me get my memory back. And Ally…" he stared down at her, determination overshadowing the questions still warm on her lips. When his gaze swept her flushed cheeks, a blast of raw emotion swamped her. "I need to remember. You have to help me. You're my last chance."

Two

She made a shallow choking sound then swallowed, drawing Finn's attention to the smooth skin of her throat, to the wildly throbbing pulse below the surface.

"Why?" she said faintly.

He remembered staring into the hospital mirror a month ago, recognizing his face, the features withdrawn and pale from the absence of sun and fresh air. And feeling a deep and utter sense of displacement, as if stuck between two planes of existence. A drifter. Someone belonging nowhere.

He couldn't—wouldn't—tell his woman *that*.

When he didn't answer, she tried again. "Finn?" she prompted in that *chocolate*-thick voice. "Why is this so important to you?"

A jolt of heat flared in his groin, flooring him. *For helve.* His mind was blank. Except for the lust...

He yanked away as if she'd grown fangs and bitten him, stunned at his lapse in control.

"Part of my life has gone. Wouldn't you do the same?" he said curtly.

To her credit she recovered quickly, tucking the remnants of shock back behind an expression of careful scrutiny.

"*I* would. But you…"

"Me, what?"

"The Finn I know wouldn't have come all this way for something like this," she continued cryptically.

"Something like what?"

"Digging up the past just to remember an old relationship. You don't dwell, Finn. You move on. That's what you do."

"Maybe I've changed."

She quirked up an eyebrow. "Really? So there's nothing more to this than a trip down memory lane? No reputation to keep spotless or for-the-good-of-the-company spin?"

If she'd planted a kiss square on his mouth it couldn't have thrown him more. His surprise must have shown because she sighed and placed her hands on her hips. "Start by telling me the truth, Finn. We owe each other that much."

So much for your careful planning, Finn thought grimly. What to do now? The reality wasn't scenarios and well-thought-out plans, it was Ally's defensiveness, the anger still simmering below the surface.

And her bizarre familiarity, her total certainty of his thoughts and reactions.

He took a breath and stuck a cautious toe in the water, unwilling to submerge himself completely.

"You know my father built up his business from nothing," he said. "Everything is tied up in it. And Marlene, my stepmother, will get a controlling share."

"So why don't you contest the will?"

"Nikolai made an amendment, a…" He frowned, searching for the English equivalent.

"Codicil?"

"Yes. It cuts her off completely. But we can't find it."

Finn watched her reach for her cup. As she blew on the rising steam from the rim, curls of rich chestnut hair swept forward, curtaining her face away from his scrutiny. The sudden and inexplicable desire to tuck those stray locks behind her ears sucker-punched him in the gut.

He dragged in a confused breath, astounded by his body's reaction. "I got the feeling Marlene didn't like you," he probed carefully.

"No."

"Why not?"

"Because I ruined her plans. Look, when I met you, I didn't know who you were. You never fully explained until we landed in Denmark, but that didn't stop your friends and family thinking I was only after your money. You were—are—a corporate wonder, Finn. A celebrity in your homeland." She flicked him a glance. "And when your stepmother told me the truth—"

"What did she tell you?"

"That we wouldn't last. That you were engaged before you left for Australia. That I should go quietly and take her money as compensation."

Finn absorbed the second stab of betrayal with outward calm, slowly swallowing his fury. "Did you—?"

"I didn't take her money."

Her quiet admission, full of conviction, instinctively told him she was telling the truth. He nodded, relieved. "I'm sorry about that."

She shot him a look of wide-eyed disbelief over the teacup, as if he'd suddenly sprouted a third eye or something.

"Can you really not remember? Anything?" she ventured.

"No."

"Not our wedding? How we met? Our…" She flushed. "Arguments?"

"Nothing."

"Wow. How do you feel here, now?"

"Weird."

"Just weird?"

"It's…disturbing," he amended. "Like I've caught you spying. You know practically everything about me and I…" He paused, then said softly, "Apart from a few flashes, I don't remember you at all."

The half truth clenched his muscles into a tight, tense knot. It must have registered on his face because her wary expression softened.

"I'm sorry about your dad," she said gently. "Did he… suffer?"

He didn't want to think about that, but the sudden pain forced a sharp breath out, tightened the muscles in his chest. "He was fine when he got to hospital, which was when I believe he wrote the codicil. The next day he had an aneurysm and never recovered."

"Oh. He is—was—" she stumbled here, blinking quickly "—a good man. I liked him." Even though she smiled, it was a fleeting one, one full of sadness.

"I thought… Marlene told me—"

"That we'd hardly spoken? That we didn't get on? Or that we got on a little *too* well?"

Finn said nothing, waiting as she shook her head in disbelief.

"He was a charmer. Said I made him feel young again. I remember…" She swallowed then plowed on. "I remember one day—he skipped out on a meeting to take me to Tivoli. We'd been in Copenhagen two weeks and he was surprised you hadn't shown me the sights yet."

"I was probably working."

"Yes," she echoed.

Irritated with her agreement but unsure why, he said, "So Marlene was jealous." When she shrugged, he raised his eyebrows. "If you're being vague to spare my feelings, then don't. I know what Marlene is capable of."

Even given a green light, she still squirmed on the couch. Finally she settled on, "Nikolai was fun. A charismatic, attractive flirt with a wicked sense of humor. But he was also my father-in-law. Marlene didn't see it that way and accused me of…well, you get the picture."

Another piece of the puzzle fell into place. It did look damning, especially in the face of Nikolai's will and Ally's controlling interest. He had to know. "Was there any truth to—"

Before he had a chance to finish, she snapped to her feet, her face flushed with anger. "Oh, my— No! *NO!*"

"Marlene's made her stance perfectly clear."

"I'll bet she has." Ally brushed her hair away from her face with one angry swipe.

"And then there's your apartment."

She frowned. "We talked about property values in Sydney, I said beachside blocks are always in demand. He bought it as an investment. When I came home I had nowhere to stay so he offered me a place for free for as long as I needed. I wanted to pay, so we agreed on a monthly rent—too low, in my opinion, but…"

Under Finn's sudden silence, she added sarcastically, "There were no secret meetings, no unchaperoned visits. Everything was aboveboard, Finn. I was in love with *you.* And Nikolai's first priority wasn't cheating on his wife, it was Sørensen Silver. Just like it was—is—yours. His dedication and driving force made it into a multinational company." She said that with an almost sad inflection. Yet it only confirmed what he already knew.

The truth of who he'd been sat uncomfortably on his shoulders: a man driven to prove himself, to follow in his father's footsteps. A man who worked too much and enjoyed the fruits of his labor too little. A man who let his wife—a woman he loved, apparently—walk out of his life.

The enormity of the task suddenly swamped him. *For helve,* how could this work? How could he overcome his wife's unconcealed distrust, save the company *and* keep this sudden unwanted attraction under wraps?

Control was slipping from his grasp and that horrified him.

The truth. She wants the truth. You have to tell her something.

He rubbed his chin with the palm of his hand. "How much did I tell you about my family?"

"Not much. I heard about the lineage from Nikolai. Louisa talked about the company, her job and the employees, plus her current boyfriend. And Marlene…besides detailing your ex-girlfriends, which she always preempted with, 'you need to know,' she had as little to do with me as possible."

Damn the woman. "My stepmother came from a poor family and has always been obsessed with money and position. She mentions 'royal blood' to anyone who'll listen, but my ancestors come from an obscure line. I'm no prince." His thinned his lips. "I broke off my engagement before I left for Sydney. The Sørensens are one of the oldest families in Denmark but with little collateral. My father tied everything up in the business. He took some risky ventures, ones that had just started to make a profit. My uncle, on the other hand, was self-made and on his death five years ago it went to me. My current worth is well over a couple of billion."

"Dollars?"

At his nod she blinked, shock sending her back a step. "I never knew."

He shrugged as if it was no big deal but that only seemed to alarm her.

Her hands began to shake. Swiftly he plucked the cup from her fingers and placed it on the table.

She made it to the couch, sat heavily and ran her fingers through her hair, tugging on the roots in frustration.

Finn knew exactly how she felt because he'd been battling with conflicting emotions for the past few months.

"Say something," he said softly, hating how he almost sounded pleading. Vulnerable.

"Give me a minute here."

So he did.

He studied her in silence, trying to compare her in-the-flesh reality with the old photos he still had. He'd stared at them for hours on end, desperately trying to recall any scrap of feeling, emotion or passion he'd obviously felt.

Nothing.

A tidal wave of remembrance washed over him now, dragged him unwillingly back to the day he'd discovered that box full of memories in his basement.

He'd sifted through the letters with those ants scuttling up his neck. And the confusion, the surety that something wasn't right, had increased. Like playing a game of hot and cold, he'd been icy standing at the basement door. Sitting on the floor surrounded by cards, letters and small gifts from a complete stranger, he was burning up.

And then came the brief flashes—an unfamiliar city skyline. A knowing look from dark-gray eyes. And the remnants of a gentle touch that seared his skin, as arousing as it was inexplicably sad.

A small light had shone weakly in the black hole of his memory. Foolishly he'd let hope bloom.

Yet after he'd reached the bottom of the box and

repacked it, the days had dragged by with no further enlightenment in sight.

Impatience had morphed into a frustration so deep his concentration was shot. He suffered flashbacks in his sleep—on the rare occasions he *did* sleep. He'd lost weight. The headaches became one big constant throb.

A week later his father had finally died. He'd tried to bury himself in the codicil mess, yet even when he'd been elbow-deep in interviews and paperwork, he'd catch a familiar scent of perfume, or hear a woman laugh a certain way. Or more frustratingly, an unconnected memory would invade his brain, waving from the sidelines but never fully revealing itself.

He couldn't live like that.

For the millionth time since the accident, he squeezed his eyes shut and repeated the words that had become his mantra: *Why can I not remember?*

Faced with this too-silent woman on the couch, all his doubts came bobbing to the surface like a buoy on the Nyhavn Canal. He'd been so focused on finding the codicil he'd shoved all those bittersweet recollections from his mind. But the questions couldn't be ignored. Why had she left? Why had he let her? And, more importantly, who *was* she? Would she sell off her shares to spite him? Or want a piece of the action?

There was only one person who could provide those answers. One woman who was now so deathly silent that Finn felt the burning desire to check her for signs of life.

Or was it a burning desire just to touch her?

He shoved his itchy fingers into his pockets as the gentle throbbing reminder of a headache began to beat.

Ally stood abruptly. "So Marlene gets control if you don't find the codicil."

"*Ja.*"

As she slowly rubbed her temple, Finn zeroed in on those

long, elegant fingers. Her nails were neatly filed and painted a screaming shade of hot pink.

"Nikolai was talking of divorce when I took over the vice presidency," he said, remembering how Louisa had put him straight on the two-faced plottings of his stepmother. "She wanted half of everything. Now she wants to sell off his company. Put thousands of people out of work. Stop financial support of a dozen charities. She'd love to see his memory in ruins and his money in her pockets. She tried to publish a tell-all book, but we got an injunction."

He eased back against the desk and reached for his cup of coffee, leaving Ally to absorb that revelation.

Partly to rid himself of this irritating pull he felt, he picked apart her features and ruthlessly analyzed them.

She was a far cry from typical Danish beauty. He could name a dozen women who were taller, slimmer, prettier.

Yet…she had a way about her, an aura that separated the pretty from the standouts. Her looks were cute rather than drop-dead gorgeous. And those abundant curves were packed into a compact five foot three, and even more abundant hair only complemented her lushness.

That hair now gently curled down her back, the shorter strands framing a determined jaw. She was more rounded than the woman in his photos. Even though her collarbone was clearly defined and her shoulders and arms toned, her figure was…well, he'd never seen someone fill a pair of blue jeans so snugly. Her hips flared out, her bottom was deliciously curved. The worn denim cupped all her assets like a loving hand.

And a million times in the past, he'd made love to her.

His body jolted, as if it subconsciously recognized the stranger in his room. As if it remembered her touch, her breath. The way her skin felt underneath his fingers. As if it longed to be buried in her earthy warmth once again.

He scowled. He'd been without a woman since the accident—a rarity, his friends had teased. But he'd felt not one shred of attraction, no sexual urges.

Another time, another place, and Ally McKnight would have been a fantasy come true. But nothing was familiar, nothing clear-cut. And his sudden attraction to a stranger just muddied the waters more.

He'd already seen flashes of his past by reading her letters. If he could regain it all… He closed his eyes briefly then opened them. He'd pinned his hopes on her and he wasn't leaving until he had answers.

And now, staring at her profile almost hidden under a wild mass of hair, he wished he could crawl into that cute little head and read her thoughts.

Finally she met his eyes and the sheer panic in hers threw him more soundly than any mind-reading could have achieved.

Before she had a chance to open her mouth and destroy his plans, he said suddenly, "Are you seeing someone?"

She choked out a harsh laugh. "A bit late to be asking that, isn't it?"

"Are you?"

"No."

"What about Tony?"

"What about him?" She narrowed her eyes.

"You called me Tony when I rang."

Ally felt like lying. She really wanted to. But instead she found herself saying, "He's just a good friend."

At his frank disbelief she rolled her eyes. "Oh, for heavens' sakes! Tony's gay, okay? G-A-Y."

"So there's no one?"

"I don't have time for a relationship."

"So what's the problem?"

She felt the blood rush to her face, angry, hot. "You can't

just drop this bombshell then expect me to fall over myself to help you. Our marriage is over."

His steely stare engulfed her like a lick of flaming heat. A cold expression bloomed across his face, distorting it until Ally finally recognized the look, knew she was seeing the aftermath of their breakup all over again.

"So," he said, menacingly soft. "This is about retribution."

Panic roiled up in her stomach and she choked on the bitter taste in her mouth. "It's about self-preservation." She stalked over to the desk and scooped up her keys.

"Where are you going?" he demanded.

"Home," she said, avoiding his eyes. "I'm tired and angry and upset. I might not have a perfect life but it's *mine*. You're obviously not prepared to hear the truth from me. And I don't know if I even *want* to help you."

And she slammed out the door.

Three

The next morning, after a half-hour power walk, Ally jumped into the shower and cranked the water up, sighing in relief as the spray pounded the tension from her aching back muscles.

The relief was short-lived as she remembered last night.

So there's no one?

I don't have time for a relationship.

She sighed and ducked her head under the spray. Her excuse tipped the predictable scale into orbit. In reality, Finn had been her whole world and when she'd left she'd cut her heart out. Loving him had meant pain, disappointment and regret. She couldn't go through all that a second time.

And boy, she'd fallen fast and hard. He'd been an unattainable, indulgent fantasy, exuding an air of supreme confidence, as if he knew and accepted his place in society, the life he was born into. Before she'd found out who he really was, she had sensed Finn was someone special. And she'd wanted to be part of that specialness, too. He was charmed and charming, so out of her reach…yet amazingly, he'd wanted her. They had quickly fallen into bed, and in the haze of intense sexual compatibility, he'd proposed. She'd accepted without hesitation, without an inkling as to how her life would change so completely.

Finn always made her body sing with one touch, one kiss. How could you go back to mediocrity after sampling perfection?

So she'd stuffed all her feelings, all her longings, deep down inside where the agonizing memories couldn't get at her.

Which was probably why it had been so easy for her ex-boss to corner her at the New Year's Eve cruise, to coax her into one of the dark suites and get her half undressed before she'd come to her senses and escaped. After she'd analyzed the situation to death, she put her lack of judgment down to pure loneliness. Simon's pursuit had made her feel attractive again and she'd wanted to prove she hadn't imagined the magic she'd shared with Finn, that she wasn't defective or weird or pining for the impossible. That she could eventually enjoy sex with another man again, even get remarried.

She gave a twisted grimace.

The very next week the office gossip grapevine had been buzzing with her and Simon's "affair." So when he'd attempted to pick up where he'd left off, she'd told him about her pregnancy. He'd shown his true colors quickly, resorting first to insults then threatening a demotion. Furious, she'd thrown his precious Walkley Award on the floor and smashed it with his nine-hundred-dollar oversized five iron. Then she'd quit.

Ally winced at the memory. She hated losing control. It made her feel…helpless. As though she was seven years old again, hearing her father blame the drink, the loan sharks, her mother. Everyone but himself. And later on, her mother promising her the moon and stars before leaving the very next day.

Her chest tightened as a thousand dark thoughts raced through her mind. What if she was her mother's daughter and couldn't cope with a child? Or worse, if she was her father all over again?

She stroked her stomach, letting the water stream over her shoulders and pool into her cupped hand resting just below her belly button.

She wouldn't let that happen. Finn may not want a child but *she* did. This baby would be wanted. Unconditionally loved.

Which meant the father could not know.

Ally got out of the shower, padded into her bedroom and finished toweling off, going over what she was going to tell Finn.

The proud, unforgiving man she'd loved.

She pulled on her underpants and clipped on a lacy pink bra.

Strange, but there'd been nothing proud or unforgiving in the way he'd asked for her help. More oddly, he'd actually let her walk out on an argument. That never happened. Usually, he pushed and twisted her words until she finally gave up. On more than one occasion, he'd shamelessly exploited their heightened emotions to kiss the fight out of her.

Her breath caught and rattled around in her throat. *Thank heavens for small mercies.*

Finally dressed, she glanced at the clock. Seven-thirty. Plenty of time to check her e-mail, do some digging on the Internet, then face her past for the last time.

Ally had called Finn and given him a half-hour warning of her arrival. She hadn't detected any overt emotion in his smooth response, no deep meaningful revelation that would indicate how she should act when they were face-to-face.

She drove down Coogee Bay Road to Finn's hotel, the window low and the CD player cranked up. Music for courage, she'd decided. More precisely, the disco remix of Gloria Gaynor's "I Will Survive." She was still humming the tune when she rode the elevator up to Finn's floor.

He stood at the door, waiting for her. For one second Ally took in the dark circles under his eyes, his travel-weary expression combined with rumpled hair, and nearly gave in to the temptation to hug him.

She pulled herself up short when he smiled, his shadows scattering along with her lapse in strength. Her gaze traveled down his body, noting the neatly pressed dress shorts and the vaguely familiar gray T-shirt.

She stared at the dips and bulges of his chest through the fabric and her memory twigged.

That T-shirt had been part of his thirtieth birthday present from her. She closed her eyes briefly as the memories sent her pulse rocketing. They'd won a packet at the Las Vegas tables and had celebrated by making love on the fiftieth-floor balcony of the Mirage.

Damn. Why isn't amnesia catching?

She swallowed thickly. *"Goddag."*

His smile was pleasant surprise. "You remember *Dansk.*"

Ally shrugged as he stepped aside to let her enter. "Just the basics."

He gestured to the breakfast tray emitting a gentle plume of delicious-smelling steam on the dining table.

"Hungry?"

"I'm not staying." She walked past him, carefully avoiding contact. A mean feat because he was just so damned... muscular, she realized. He'd been working out. Sweating. Groaning. Heaving...

She headed toward the open patio doors. The sun streamed in, dappling the carpet in shards of brilliant light. The familiar toot and hum of traffic rose up from the street, a gentle background soundtrack to the ever-present crashing waves.

She breathed in deeply before turning to face him. "I just wanted to tell you face to face. I can't do this."

"Why not?"

"For a million reasons. Starting with letting the past stay buried."

"I thought this might happen," he said shortly. "So I'm prepared to offer monetary compensation."

"Excuse me?"

"How much? How much will it take for your help?"

"Did you think...? Nothing!" Insulted that he'd actually considered the thought, her cheeks flared. Instinctively she took a step back, toward the door.

"Wait," he commanded. "I didn't mean it the way it sounded."

She put her hands on her hips. "And how do you think it sounded?"

"It sounded cheap. I'm sorry."

Finn apologizing again? She blinked in surprise but he'd turned to the coffee pot on the table.

"Did we hate each other that much, Ally?" he asked calmly, concentrating on pouring his coffee.

Her heart bottomed out at the underlying thread of confusion behind those words. "No. It was...quite the opposite."

He straightened and proffered a cup. "I still don't understand why you won't help me."

I can't *help you.* She took the cup and carefully avoided his fingers. There had been times when she'd hated him, hated herself for the mess they'd made of their lives. But she'd gone through a multitude of changes these past few months, finally becoming grounded at the ripe age of twenty-nine. The adult Ally was telling her this would be a perfect opportunity to prove she'd moved on with her life, that he didn't affect her anymore. That she was happy and content without him.

But then she thought of her heart, still bearing the scars of their parting. And the recriminations, the rejection. The abject disappointment in him, in herself, knowing she wasn't enough to make him happy.

It took her breath away just thinking about it.

A tumble of irony threatened to erupt in a maniacal giggle. She'd been trying to forget the past and Finn had gone and beaten her to it.

"We hurt each other, Finn. It wouldn't be healthy to do this."

"And you think a hole in my memory is healthy?" He cradled his cup in one large palm and leaned against the edge of the table. "You think making a thousand employees jobless is healthy? Of losing a solid Danish export because of one woman's pettiness?"

"Don't give me a guilt trip." Ally narrowed her eyes. "That won't wash."

He sighed. "We'll be two adults sharing information. That's it."

Confusion tugged her in a thousand different directions. Ever since last night, he'd been giving off a lost-soul aura. He was different in many tiny ways, as if he'd been touched by a stranger. He didn't seem like her Finn anymore. Her Danish Viking.

Whoa. Back up. Not hers. Not anymore.

But he *was* different. She could sense that as surely as only a woman loving a man could. She could see it in the tiny nuances of his expression, his restraint. The dark shutter he'd thrown over his thoughts.

His mannerisms had once been a journey of discovery, giving her an enormous glow of womanly pride when she'd figured them out. He was an elegant, confident vision of

Danish wealth and style, a man she was sure would never look twice at a middle-class Mick from the western suburbs. Now he was almost approachable. Those new lines on his face showed him as a flesh-and-blood man rather than the powerful businessman he was. Not the smart, connected Finn Jakob Sørensen, Denmark's fifth-richest bachelor and the shining star of Sørensen Silver.

Her Internet search had revealed more than he'd ever told her, of a pampered, educated life, which had been going from strength to strength until that tragic accident merely days after she'd left. Meanwhile hers had ground to a painful screeching halt. Their union had even been reduced to one sentence: "After a brief marriage, Denmark's favorite son is currently single."

But that wasn't the part that really hurt. If their love *had* been as unique and spectacular as she had once thought, surely Finn would have remembered just one tiny thing about her?

For some inexplicable reason, that thought made her want to crawl into a ball and cry.

She glanced down at her cup, sniffed at the contents. Strawberry tea. She took a sip and nearly scalded her tongue.

"What can I do that doctors can't?" she finally asked.

"When I went through your letters, I remembered things."

"But you don't have any of my letters," she said, confused.

"They were in my basement."

Unable to explain that, Ally let it go. "Surely you've been to therapy, had tests…"

"The best money can buy. They all say the same thing—wait and see what happens."

"Ah."

He gave her a sharp look. "What's that supposed to mean?"

"Patience is not your strong point."

A strange expression clouded his face, as if he'd caught her with a hand in the till. She let it slide. "So the memory loss isn't permanent?"

"The doctors don't know." She could hear how he hated the not knowing. "I could either regain full memories, or bits and pieces. Or nothing at all. They described it as having a lot of—what do you call it? Day...day jar..."

"Déjà vu."

"That's it. So—" He shoved a hand through his hair, a look of fierce determination in his direct gaze. "Tell me what I can do to convince you, Ally."

Her name curled off his tongue in that delicious accent she never got sick of hearing. It had whispered words of passion and hot sex, declared undying love.

And coolly shattered all her rose-colored dreams of family and security.

She shook her head in anguish and his confidence flattened into a frown.

"If I can't have you willing, Ally, then you leave me no option."

Her heart plummeted. *He's going to kick me out of the apartment.* "Why are you doing this?"

"Believe me, *lille skat,* I don't want it to be this way."

His rough confession faltered her breath as the hard sculptured planes of his face softened.

Ally carefully placed her cup on the table. *Walk out. It wouldn't be hard. You did it once, you can do it again. Find yourself a lawyer and battle it out.*

But just as she was about to follow through on that thought, he sighed. A sigh full of frustration and missed opportunity and things not coming out right.

A sigh that got her square in the chest.

"'You're the true reason the sun burns so bright...'"

She stiffened, her entire body tense with shock.

My poem.

Her gaze flew to him and locked, green on gray. His expression was one of familiar stubbornness and resolve. Completely unapologetic.

Silently she begged him to stop, to take it back, but her mouth was as paralyzed as the rest of her body. She couldn't do anything but numbly listen to the words she knew off by heart.

"'…the steady flame shining in the blackest of night. The joy in my life, the smile on my face.'"

"Stop," she finally whispered. But Finn was intent on ignoring her. He merely arched an eyebrow, a challenge in his eyes. It sent danger whispering along her skin and she wasn't game enough to march over there and physically stop him.

"'When my heart was the prize you didn't even need to race.'"

Ally crossed her arms, steeling herself against the battery of emotion that came with every word Finn recited. But the memories, like tiny hailstones, rained down, striking against her resolve with a tiny *chink.*

"'A bright burning summer turned melancholy blue. Believe in the strength of every 'I love you.' Have faith in me please, when all is said and done. We'll be together forever, two hearts rejoined as one,'" Finn concluded.

Silence fell like a thick cloud.

It was a silence in which Ally could hear the thump of her heart forcing blood to her head. A silence punctuated by the flutter of the patio curtains, the distant crash and pound of waves from the beach twenty stories below, the honk and rev of street traffic. It was a silence that really wasn't one at all because it was full of noisy thoughts.

Oh Lord. She wasn't made of stone. Nor was her heart. If it was, she wouldn't have agreed to see him despite her grave misgivings. She wouldn't have heard him out. And she wouldn't be feeling this overwhelming sadness for what he had lost.

For the past few months she'd tried to make herself not care.

Unable to meet his penetrating gaze any longer, she squeezed her eyes tightly shut, afraid he could see the raw emotion behind her expressionless facade, detect the tremble in her chin.

She'd come here to tell him he was asking for more than she could give. But she had a niggling feeling that if she didn't help him when he was vulnerable and in desperate need, she'd regret it for the rest of her life.

The man who now stood before her was an enigma. He had drunk long and hard from the well of tragedy, had tasted heartache just like her. Outwardly he still looked like the Finn she knew, had that same you-know-you-want-me pull, possessed that same hot stare that made her believe she was the only desirable woman on the planet. But he now had ghosts. Emotional scars.

And she quite possibly held the key to unlocking his memory.

If she refused him, he might never recover the past. And that realization—that she was now the only one who had experienced the bliss and heartache of their union—made her feel horribly, terribly alone.

What kind of mother would I be if I turned my back on someone in need? Refused to help the father of my child?

Her heart ached. It was tempting to take those few steps between uncertainty and freedom. But she couldn't shake the responsibility that lay before her—of families and children who would suffer because of her decision.

It was a responsibility she couldn't run away from this time.

When she finally looked up, the expression in his eyes blew her away. Eyes once so full of passion and utter certainty of his destiny were now so…empty.

He could never fully verbalize what his eyes revealed. It was the look of a man who'd tried everything, and who was now down to his last option.

With a semblance of control slowing her breath, Ally said slowly, "You memorized my poem."

That all-seeing gaze never left her face, pinning her to the spot. "From what I can recall before the accident, no one's ever written me poetry before."

Inside, it felt as if her guts had been scooped out with an ice cream spoon. Outwardly, she went for a nonchalant shrug. "Love does strange things to people. I wrote corny poetry."

"Tell me that meant nothing to you just now."

"It meant nothing to me just now."

"Liar."

He crossed the room in two strides, backing her up against the window. Her bottom hit the glass with a soft thump as she tried to inch away from his sudden heat. Her whole body leaped to life and she felt the tingle of anticipation right up to the roots of her hair.

And right down to her stomach that churned like a blender on high.

With more bravado than sense, she stood her ground. "That's not fair."

"The accident wasn't fair. My memory loss wasn't fair. Some things in life aren't." At this angle she had to look up to meet his eyes. And wished she hadn't. They were full of an emotion she didn't care to remember, tinged with a sexual awareness she could hardly forget. "I'm not a man prone to flowery speeches, Ally. The woman who wrote that poem was a woman in love. Think about what we used to have and help me find that codicil. Please."

With that one tiny word she stifled a frustrated groan, knowing there was no way on God's earth she could refuse him now, knowing how much swallowed pride it took him to ask for help.

He made a move, almost as if he was going to touch her but then thought better of it.

"I'm as close to begging as you'll get me, Ally. There will be nothing personal in it. If it makes you feel any better—" his smile was as cool as a stranger's "—I'll be on my best behavior. I won't even touch you."

But what if I want *you to touch me?* She searched his face, looking for just one iota of recognition. The emerald-green eyes that stared back held none.

Finn needed her. His words admitted it. His eyes confirmed it. And his actions—although disturbingly out of character—backed up his story.

He was…she was…

Excited by that.

This powerful, amazing man depended on her, and it stunned her to know that she wanted him needing her.

"I'll do it."

His smile was triumphant, all potent male in the face of victory. And there it was again, that pull, that sexual connection like a living entity, swamping her body, tempting her to sin.

A shiver of excitement goose-bumped her arms as she quickly shoved her mounting panic down with a firm hand. She wasn't a slave to her hormones. She could switch everything off and handle it like a responsible, mature adult.

Right?

Four

It took all of Finn's hard-won control to swallow his whoop of triumph and resist planting a kiss on her upturned mouth.

His insides tossed with a disturbing mix of victory and foreboding as he battled to leash his exhilaration.

When the plane had banked into Sydney air space, circling past the world-famous bridge and the white sails of the Sydney Opera House lit by a thousand nightlights, he'd made a promise to himself: do anything it took to recover his memory so he could save the company. He'd been fully prepared to lie to get her compliance. Now, he was shocked—appalled, even—that he'd been prepared to go that far.

"Thank you," he said simply, swallowing the bitter taste of self-disgust.

"You're welcome."

Like that stupid no-touching promise, her tentative smile only succeeded in escalating his pulse.

Deliberately he backed off and walked over to the breakfast tray, feeling as if he'd just increased that space to football-field proportions. His body groaned, but his head congratulated his iron control, control that had taken a battering a mere minute ago.

She was too tempting, standing there giving off all those vulnerable vibes. Her wide gray eyes could probe a man's soul, dig out all his secrets without an ounce of effort.

He hadn't expected to feel this kind of wild inexplicable attraction to a total stranger, hadn't expected his body to start acting like a horny teenager's.

And hadn't expected to feel like such a *lort* for forcing her into this situation.

"The food's getting cold." He refused to look up, as if somehow she could have detected his deception. So he busied himself with the cutlery, releasing the cover from the breakfast plate with a rush of fragrant steam. "You want some toast? Some fruit? I ordered for us both."

Fully expecting her to refuse, he was surprised by her quick nod. "Okay."

In a strange mockery of domestic bliss they sat at the long dining table and ate their meal in silence, waiting for the other to speak and set the tone of their impending partnership.

But a minute later he could have cleaved the air with a butter knife, the only sound the clink of cutlery on plate. Rather than calm the awkwardness, the low rumble of crashing waves outside only intensified it.

With a clatter that sounded like a shot he put his fork down. "So where do you want to start?"

Ally blinked, took a breath and attempted a businesslike expression to hide her nervousness. "Well, I have a few conditions."

His eyebrow kinked up speculatively. "Go on."

"I want my letters back. All of them."

He paused then nodded. "Okay."

"You sign those divorce papers."

"Done."

A little miffed he'd agreed so readily, Ally added, "And my apartment block. I gather you own it now?"

He had the good grace to look uncomfortable. "Not personally, *nej*. It's part of Sørensen Silver's assets."

"So you lied."

"*Ja.*"

"Well, that will cost you." His eyes narrowed in suspicion but Ally was past caring. "I want the deed to my place."

His scowl was disapproval enough. She tilted her chin up. "Take it or leave it, Finn. You can get the contract drawn up while we tackle your problem. And no more lies."

"We should—"

"Please, let me finish." She glanced away, down the hallway, her gaze landing on the open bedroom door barely visible. To the bed beyond that.

Rumpled covers. The smell of his sleep-tousled body between the cotton sheets. Him kissing her awake and making sweet love…

Her groin started to throb. *Arrggh.*

"What happens if this doesn't work?" she said.

"It will."

"But what if it doesn't?" she persisted.

His expression told her he wouldn't settle for that option. "We'll cross that river when we come to it."

"Bridge," she corrected, falling into their intimate habit before she could stop herself.

"*Unskuld?*"

"The phrase is *cross that bridge*. How long are you planning to stay?"

"Two months. Until the end of May."

Painful memories rushed in as her stomach bottomed out. *Never thought I'd feel* that *kick in the guts again.* "Because I have deadlines to meet. A life." *Without you.* The unsaid words hung between them, cold and stark. He didn't look happy. "I know you want answers," she continued calmly. "I appreciate that. But I have other commitments. I have work to do."

"What do you do?"

"I'm a writer."

"Who for?"

"Until last week, *Bliss* magazine. Now I'm freelance. I'm working on a book."

Finn leaned forward in his chair and she instinctively pulled back. "You misunderstand me, Ally. I will do anything it takes to make this work. Even waiting for you to meet your commitments…within reason."

His conviction stole the snappy comeback from her lips.

"Do you have photos of us? Letters?" He reached for his cup, watching her with unnerving scrutiny.

"Yes. They're in a box under a pile of other useless—" She snapped her mouth shut, too late.

His eyes flashed, the only indication of his displeasure. "We'll need them today."

"You know, you're still as bossy as I remember," she blurted out.

"Correct me if I'm wrong. You agreed to do this. You have letters, photos and other pieces from our past."

"Right."

"So what," he said with exaggerated patience, "is the problem?"

Ally wanted to throw her now-cold tea in his face. Instead she said curtly, "I have a deadline. Next week, to be exact. You'll have to cut me a little slack."

"Fint."

She nearly flinched at his clipped tone. He had her compliance and now he was freezing her out with an icy stare and one cold word. It still managed to drop her heart to her feet.

They cleared the table in another stretch of silence. When there was finally nothing left to do, Finn turned to her.

"Why did you save those letters?"

Because I'm a sentimental fool. With warm guilt flushing her cheeks she said, "My… I lost everything in a house fire when I was ten. So when I can, I save my memories."

His eyes softened with sympathy and Ally swallowed. *No. No, don't look like that. I don't want your pity.*

"That must've been tough."

Her chin tilted up. "Yeah." On the pretense of getting a drink of water, she went over to the kitchenette.

Finn followed. "Tell me about our wedding."

The out-of-the-blue question took her aback. *Prepare yourself, Ally. There'll be a lot more.*

"We met in Sydney in April. A month later you convinced me to go backpacking through Europe. Greece, Italy, Portugal. The UK. Six months later we ended up in Las Vegas. We were married on your birthday at The Little Chapel of Love." She couldn't help a small smile at the memories. "We had an Elvis impersonator and he serenaded us with a 'Hunk o' Burning Love'…" They had laughed so freely, so easily. They'd been so focused, so intent on each other. So in love. She'd never suspected anything was wrong.

Her smile fell quicker than a shooting star.

"So our marriage wasn't all bad," he probed.

"Some of it was…wonderful."

She reached for the water jug and poured. When she lifted the glass to her lips, she eyed his reflection through the mirrored wall which was artfully arranged behind glass shelving. He was leaning against the counter with arms crossed, a potent mix of curiosity and masculine sexuality.

She swallowed and suddenly his eyes were all over her throat, taking in every miniscule movement. Desperate for something to do, she abruptly placed the glass in the sink and turned on the faucet. As she rinsed the glass, she studied the rivulets on her skin, as if they held the key to finding the courage to withstand the days—possibly weeks—ahead.

"Which parts were wonderful?" His voice came out deceptively smooth and controlled.

"Sex."

A muffled sound. Like a choke. *Not so controlled.* With downcast eyes she hid a smile and continued casually, "Sex was good. Great, in fact."

"Really."

His reply was thick and husky, and with curiosity prickling her skin, she chanced a glance.

He was staring at her. At her mouth. The total focus of his gaze, the desire flaming his eyes, hit her square in the stomach, winding her. The air suddenly got sucked from the spacious kitchenette and shrunk it down to microscopic proportions.

She swallowed but it didn't help. "Yes," she managed to croak out. "We were—"

His eyes imprisoned hers. "I think I get the picture."

Flushing, she reached for a towel. Part of her wished he'd just give her some space. The other part—the one rapidly overtaking common sense and self-preservation—wanted him to strip her naked and totally invade it.

"Since we're being totally honest, a few things have been bothering me," he murmured. "Like why you walked out on our marriage."

"What?" She coughed, trying to clear the rough edge to her

voice. But when he remained silent, she said slowly, "For one, you lied."

"About what?"

"You name it. Your family, your money. We spent the best part of six months together and somehow you just forget to tell me who you really are?"

A shadow crossed his face. "And do all those things matter to you?"

"No. But you shouldn't have waited until the plane had touched down at Copenhagen airport to warn me. Until those reporters chased us through the terminal, until they photographed me topless in the bathroom at your apartment the next day."

His nostrils flared, his mouth grim, but he said nothing.

"I was woefully unprepared for the stir I'd cause. I didn't want that. I couldn't handle it. Marlene was right about that."

"And so you ended it, *elskat.*" His voice came in dangerously low, almost like a caress. "Without any discussion or explanation. You walked out on our marriage, out on *me* just like that?"

She pulled herself up to her full five foot three, felt the unyielding marble counter at her back. "You changed once we got to Denmark. You became another person. We'd lost that spark of enjoyment somehow and went from newlyweds to complete strangers in two weeks."

Her expression tightened. "I asked you a dozen times to go to counseling with me, to get our relationship some help, but you said there was nothing wrong. I always felt it was my fault—I wasn't flexible enough, understanding enough. But I always had to bend to your schedule and insane workload."

Refusing to meet his accusing stare any longer, she skittered her gaze over his shoulder. If he weren't only a couple of feet away, staring as if he were waiting to catch her in a lie, maybe she could be stronger. More aloof. But, to her mortification, she felt the clogging emotion choke her throat. Furiously she blinked until control was in her firm grasp. "I hated arguing, especially with you. You always had to be right, and my opinion didn't matter."

He shifted his weight and recrossed his arms, considering her with curiosity and doubt.

The familiarity of his stance—those muscular brown arms crisscrossing his wide chest, his expression full of powerful scrutiny—made her skin leap to life. She tried to ignore the potent attraction but it was becoming impossible. Her body knew him intimately and insisted on reminding her at every opportunity.

She sighed and straightened the towel on the rail. "You didn't let on, but I could feel what you were thinking—that we'd made a huge mistake. You worked too much, we argued all the time. Your family hated me and thought you'd married me just to shock them—an accusation you never denied. I was just so tired of fighting. I wanted peace for once."

When he stepped inside her comfort zone all her nerves went on high alert. *If he can be this close and not feel this…our…my hunger for him—surely I must be imagining it?*

Finn noticed that she stubbornly refused to meet his gaze, instead staring into the sink, seemingly fascinated by the remnants of water clinging to the basin. It also tipped her hair across her face, hiding her expression.

It made her appear shy. A deadly combination of innocence and lush touch-me curves. As if the burden of the world's troubles were on her shoulders, breathing down her neck.

She turned him on quicker than a deep hot kiss just before dawn. More disturbingly, he found all his primitive desires stampede ahead, relegating common sense to the back of his mind.

Yet her revelation, tinged with barely restrained hurt, cut like a razor-sharp blade. It poked and prodded, drawing a trickle of guilt until his thoughts tumbled together into one big blur.

Unable to help himself, he gently placed a hand on her shoulder. She jumped. *So nervous.*

Slowly he touched her chin, turning her to face him, then brushed his fingers against her cheek. *So soft.*

Her gaze, wide-eyed and panicky, snapped to his. *So scared.*

"What about your no-touching rule?" she got out.

Rebuffed, he pulled back. "Right. Bad idea."

Ally flushed. He said that way too quickly, as if it was the most stupid thing he'd ever done. Was she that undesirable? Resistible? *Don't say it, don't say it, don't say...*

"You never used to think so." *Damn. You said it.*

His eyebrows rose in a silent question.

"We had chemistry. We spent most of our time in bed." The burning on her cheeks intensified as she tried for a worldly shrug. It felt stiff and a little fake.

"Really?" he asked.

"Really."

His lips curved and her irritation flared into peevish anger. Did he think she was making it up? Or throwing down some sort of gauntlet? Now wouldn't that be ironic? She crossed her arms as a bevy of fluttering hit her low in the belly.

Partly because he couldn't help himself and partly because her angry gray eyes seemed to be daring him, Finn tested the softness of her cheek again with gentle fingertips.

Her skin was smooth and warm, and suddenly he wondered what she felt like in other, intimate places. This close he could make out the faint dusting of freckles hugging the bridge of her nose. This close he could see she wore no makeup. But then, she didn't need it. Her eyes were wide and as dark as a Danish winter's day just before snowfall, her mouth lush and inviting, curved up at the corners as if she was enjoying a secret joke or an intimate memory.

A memory…it flashed by so quickly he barely had time to grab it, to imprint it in his brain before it vanished. Foggy and unclear, like an unfocused camera, he saw Ally smiling, her eyes full of love and desire. And in that memory she bent forward and kissed him so tenderly it hitched his breath, struck him down like a penalty shot to the stomach.

He wasn't aware he'd leaned in until he felt her warm breath feather across his mouth, her tiny gasp of shock parting those teasing lips.

"What was the other thing bothering you?" Her voice came out slightly breathy, as if she'd run too quickly up the stairs. It snared something deep and primal and possessive inside. This woman was his. He'd made her his.

And, heaven help him, he wanted to make her his all over again.

Five

Finn yanked away. "Nothing."

Battling to contain a dozen raw urges simmering below the surface, he stormed into the living area as if a pack of wolf-hounds were snapping at his heels. *Now who's lying?* Of course he wanted to touch her. What red-blooded male wouldn't? And those lips. That body. That hair...

A sharp prickling started on his neck, oozed down his back. An image flashed, of Ally lying naked on a four-poster bed, her wrists bound by black silk scarves and a mischievous look in her eyes.

Blood pounded to his groin again. Shards of pain stabbed in his head and he groaned, grinding the heel of his hands into his eyes. It did no good. The image lingered, and now her smell was in his nostrils, his mouth. Everywhere. That teasing scent coupled with the musky-skinned flame of arousal. He could feel the silken heat of her skin beneath his hands, the erotic pucker of her rosy nipples. Taste the sweetness of the sensitive flesh as he took one in his mouth and sucked.

He released his breath in one forceful hiss, stumbling. Bracing himself with the back of a chair, he fought, breathless, against the barrage of fractured memories crowding his mind.

Ah, her voice, husky with passion, begging him to stop, to let her touch him. And his answering laugh, full of wicked male confidence, telling her to wait her turn.

Then the scene abruptly shattered.

He felt as if he'd been tackled by an entire soccer team. He took two staggering breaths and tried to swallow, but his throat was dry and scratchy. Sweat beaded along his forehead and he impatiently swiped it from his eyes.

He heard Ally's footsteps behind him and whirled. "Did I ever tie you up?"

"Excuse me?"

"When we had sex. Did I ever tie you to the bed?"

The intake of breath hissed gently between her teeth. "Are you trying to embarrass—"

"You think this is a game to me?"

Ally slowly swallowed in the face of his blazing expression. "I don't know. Is it?"

When his eyes narrowed, impending danger suddenly replaced the indignation hammering in her lungs.

"If I were playing some sort of seduction game," he drawled smoothly, "I'd go about it…something like…this…"

Ally jumped as he took one determined step forward.

"You're naked."

His words hung like a blunt challenge in the air. Through her shock, she watched his mouth twist into sexy knowledge. Fascinated, she couldn't tear herself away, he the predator and she a deer caught in his singular gaze.

"Tied to a four-poster bed."

He took another step, shoving the chair under the table with a loud scrape on the polished wood floor. Helplessly she watched his deliberate, loose-limbed stride disintegrate the space between her and freedom.

"Black silk scarves."

Another silent step…then another…until he was just an arms' reach away. She smelled the faint tang of his cologne, heard the shallow breath from his lips that told her he was teetering on the brink of control. His face was flushed and taut, those eyes bled to almost black, the look in them…naked wanting.

The realization struck her full force, as though the moon had crashed to earth and she was ground zero.

He wanted her.

He demolished the space between them to nothing, put his hands on the wall behind her head, effectively cutting off escape.

"You're moaning, all hot and sweaty," he murmured.

Ally swallowed the thrum of her heart, mesmerized by that mouth only an inch away. She could feel his warm breath on her skin, smell the arousal on it like a female scenting her mate.

"You have a freckle right here," he moved and the back of his hand skimmed briefly down the side of her left breast, "and another one here." His fingers tripped low across her belly, over the fabric of her T-shirt.

His body was so close she could feel the energy in the muscle and sinew beneath the thin barrier of clothes. His searching eyes bored into hers, reflecting arousal and the promise of much, much more, until Ally didn't think she could stand unaided for another second.

"Anything else?" she got out, her voice croaky with the buildup of anticipation. With an attempted careless gesture she flicked her hair off her too-hot neck, but his breath ended up replacing it. Shivers tripped over her sensitive skin.

"One more thing."

He grasped her chin, forcing her to look at him. Unable to meet the raw need in his eyes, hers fluttered closed as his mouth descended...only to fly back open on the end of a ragged gasp when his head dipped lower, much lower, and his hot breath and teasing lips feathered over one puckered nipple straining against her T-shirt.

"These," he murmured, transferring heat and pounding want through the thin cotton fabric, "these are magnificent."

Ally tried to take a steadying breath but it made her head spin. Then he glanced up.

Looking down into those dark passion-filled eyes proved even more dangerous. There were secrets there, ones she wasn't entirely sure she could unravel. Secrets that would hurt and scar and draw painful blood all over again.

"If you're trying to prove a point, then you've made it," Ally whispered. "I never said we weren't attracted to each other."

Abruptly his expression shut down.

"And I think you know I'm deadly serious about this, Ally." He jerked away.

One second she'd been hot and craving and the next, he'd thrown a bucket of icy reality in her face.

He strode over to the phone and barked a request down the line without so much as a glance backwards. She was thankful, because she was sure her emotions, every last tender one, were written all over her face. Frustration, confusion. And more importantly, a pounding exhilaration that felt like a neon sign plastered on her head, screaming Take Me Now!

So she pulled herself together and straightened her clothing. Made a futile attempt to cool her burning cheeks until she realized her hands were still shaking.

But when Finn hung up and turned back to her, Ally was suddenly acutely aware of what had nearly transpired. Yet he appeared completely unruffled and, for that, she swallowed her sharp retort. If he wanted to act as if a frisson of hot electricity had not sparked and nearly burned them both to a crisp, then so would she. He had always enjoyed arousing her until she was practically clawing at him to make love to her, and for once, she would not go begging like a sex-starved floozy.

He muttered something.

"Sorry?" she asked, wishing she could keep the length of the room between them forever.

"I said, that...shouldn't have happened," he said stiffly. "I apologize."

"That's the third time," she murmured, shaking her head.

"For what?"

"An apology. You never apologize."

Her firm statement plunged his brow into a frown. "Never?"

"No."

Unsure how to respond to that, Finn watched her hands go to the edge of her T-shirt and fiddle with the hem. Her unblinking eyes grazed over his face, then his lips. She frowned, the action creating a tiny valley of confusion between her eyebrows.

"What about when I was wrong?" he ventured skeptically.

"You made it a point never to be wrong."

"But what if I was?"

She shrugged, almost as if it didn't matter. "You'd buy me a gift."

"What?"

"Earrings. A necklace. A soft toy. Once you gave me an electric flower that danced in time to music."

"I gave you gifts but not an apology?"

"They're in a box in my wardrobe if you want to—"

"No!" He ran a hand through his hair and continued more calmly, "No. I believe you."

"Gee, thanks." She drew herself up as though he'd offended

her. "Look, I know this situation is strange, and I know how difficult it is to trust a complete stranger, but it'll be a lot easier if you stop doubting me. Now, let's go."

"Where?"

"We're going out."

The abrupt switch from hot wanting to businesslike cool threw him and he stood there like an idiot, dumbfounded.

And because his pride was dented and the remnants of lust still sliced at the edges of his common sense, he said, "Afraid something might happen, Ally? That I won't be able to control myself and end up ravishing you on the floor?"

Her thin smile was unamused. "You should see some of the places we saw together. To jog that memory of yours."

Ally felt the small heat of victory when she saw a flush creep up his neck.

Six

Bloody victory and its tiny lifespan, Ally cursed later as they walked through the open-air markets at The Rocks. The sky was a clear, brilliant blue, complementing the cheerful sun. Through the gaps in the old colonial heritage buildings, multicolored sails of luxury yachts floated across the harbor, adding a holiday feel to Sunday.

A Sydney ferry cleaved past, throwing up foam and spray. Sydney Harbour looked glorious under the curve of the world-famous bridge.

And she was feeling less than glorious.

Both of them silently acknowledged the danger of revisiting the shortly leashed passion nipping at their heels so they managed to keep up the pretense of not caring, instead putting their energies into their daunting task.

Finn did not touch her again. In fact, it seemed to Ally that his distance was a deliberate rebuke. Punishment. She was getting what she wanted, so why did it feel all wrong?

She'd spent the last couple of hours either in loaded expectance or running off at the mouth. She babbled about her employment history, the places they'd seen together in Sydney, all the little bits and pieces that she thought mattered.

All she got for her efforts was an occasional question or complete silence.

Beneath her nonstop commentary the tension simmered, a constant yet unspoken reminder. If Ally did accidentally brush Finn's arm—just to make sure she wasn't imagining it, of course—she felt the zing of heat in the pit of her belly, in her tender breasts. And then she was left with crowded memories and an aching longing in her groin.

Now walking under the bright canopies draped across George Street, she watched Finn wander past the stalls and keenly study the array of gifts and unusual local wares. People pressed around them, but for once Ally's mild claustrophobia dissipated as she observed Finn.

His wide back, strong shoulders, the graceful stride, the confidence. She saw people—especially the women—respond to that. A girl selling old photographs smiled flirtatiously. An older woman touched his arm in response when he asked about her art. The woman's husband chimed in with a grin and a handshake. Finn's favorite-celebrity persona was well-deserved, she thought as she watched him bestow smiles and conversation. Adoring subjects apparently weren't confined to Denmark.

She slid her gaze downward to his lean waist, then to that perfectly formed backside and muscular set of legs.

She'd loved touching him. Couldn't get enough of running her hands over his well-shaped thighs, the ridges of his stomach. Like a blind man craving the touch of recognition, she'd marveled at the dips and planes of his body. Especially his...

"Ally? You still with me?"

She snapped her gaze up to meet his direct green one and felt her whole body heat up. "Yes?"

He nodded to the piece of carved wood he held. "This looks familiar."

Reality check. "You were fascinated with aboriginal art. You couldn't get enough of it. I had to stop you after the third didgeridoo." Her smile came unbidden. "When we met, you'd just been on an outback trek with some friends."

"How *did* we meet?"

"You were helping a friend start up a courier company." She remembered the day with disturbing clarity. A powerful rainstorm. Her broken umbrella. Clapping eyes on the most gorgeously confident Danish man she'd ever seen. And to balance that confidence, he'd been perfectly charming, exuding an aura of a man in command of his future. His life. There was something regal about him that drew people's eyes and caused them to linger.

"I had to courier my boss some suits in Hawaii. He was on leave," she clarified, "with his latest entourage of bimbos. They were Armani."

"The bimbos?"

"The suits." She smothered a grin. "I told you he was cheating on his wife and you offered to lose them en route."

"The bimbos?"

"Enough about the bimbos. I'm talking about the suits!" She laughed this time, which made him laugh, too. Incredibly, she felt the gentle tug of their lost camaraderie and welcomed the lightheartedness after the morning of gut-churning angst. And when he chuckled, that warm familiar sound made her breath come out a bit quicker. "I must have a sign on my back saying 'will do anything for a paycheck.' Landing crappy bosses is my forté. The next one in the editorial department—"

Harassed then demoted me, she nearly said. Instead she finished lamely, "—was just as bad."

"So you quit."

"Yep. I hate the rigid nine-to-five thing."

"You're too creative."

She gave him a surprised smile. "I like being outside, not locked in an office all day."

"See?" He spread his hands wide. "We do agree on something."

Since when had he hated the office? "Must be a first."

He grinned, familiar creases bracketing his eyes and snagging something deep and hot inside. But her smile faltered when he leaned in to murmur, "We weren't incompatible with other things, *elskat.*"

Then he turned back to the tables, selected an intricate soapstone carving of the Harbour Bridge and studied it carefully.

Control yourself, Ally, she cautioned. *Do not touch the merchandise. Do not pass Go. Do not collect two hundred dollars.*

She suddenly felt as if she'd landed on the Go to Jail square. Permanently.

She'd been a mystery to him. He'd admitted as much on their first date. Who would've thought someone with Finn's pedigree and social circle would want Alexandra McKnight, daughter of a drunk and an irresponsible mother who'd never grown up? His stepmother had been right—she had nothing to offer that he couldn't find anywhere else.

Long-forgotten pain made her breath falter. Becoming adult Ally—calm and detached about the whole situation— would be the hardest test of her life. So if she needed to stop herself from going completely crazy, if she let impulsive Ally creep in on occasion, and imagined tracing those laugh lines, running her hands over his face…indulging in a small fantasy from the past…well, no-one would know except her.

I can do this. I will do this. Then he'll go and I'll be free.

A lump formed in her throat and it suddenly felt hard to swallow.

"How's that memory? Anything happening yet?" she asked.

He shook his head. "Not yet."

On the pretense of examining a hand-blown glass near Ally's elbow, Finn glanced at her. The knee-length denim skirt, platform sneakers and babydoll pink shirt made her look like a college student, not someone in her late twenties. But the shirt's stretchy material hugged a body that screamed *woman.* It was a shirt that flashed skin every time she reached for something. He'd found himself staring at that tiny expanse of curvy tanned waist as if she was the first woman he'd seen in ten years.

He caught a hint of scent as she leaned across the table, so close her hair brushed along his arm…something fresh and floral…before she quickly straightened.

He'd only had a brief taste of her, but like an addict he craved more. More of her skin, more of her scent. More of that silken velvet hair, which was still a riot of curls, as if he'd only just finished dragging his fingers through it.

He could see why he'd been drawn to her, why she intrigued him so much now. If his situation weren't so dire then he would have taken time just to enjoy her, to savor her.

He shook his head. Waxing poetic over a finished relationship? Damn if this situation hadn't managed to mess up his mind already.

"I've been reading up on your condition on the Internet," she said as she replaced a photo frame on the table. Her shirt settled back, covering up the source of his rapt attention. "Let's have lunch and you can tell me what you know."

He nodded, not trusting himself to speak. If he did, he might end up voicing that obscene thought that he wanted *her* for lunch.

Seven

Ally decided on the Lowenbrau Keller, a casual wine-bar restaurant with open-air tables, friendly waiters and good food. And more importantly, no memories of Finn.

Having him sitting across the table in the flesh, studying her from behind impenetrable sunglasses and haloed by the sun, was enough to handle without suffering the flashbacks, too.

After they had ordered, Finn removed his glasses and handed her a piece of paper. She took it warily. "What's this?"

"I made a list."

"Of what?"

"Questions. About us."

She slowly unfolded it and began to read.

Finn noticed the way her lashes swept down, brushing her cheeks like a pair of tiny dark fans against the apricot skin. He wondered if he'd ever kissed the smattering of dusty freckles across the bridge of her nose. Whether he'd ever compared the taste of her skin to something edible. And whether it had lived up to the promise of her scent. Lime? Mandarin? Something fresh with a hint of floral—like her hair.

Finally she laid the paper on the table. "Where'd you come up with these? Favorite food? Color? Time of year?"

Finn shrugged. "It's a starting point."

She leaned back. "Anything with pasta in it, pink and spring. And despite my best efforts, I'm not a creature of habit. I never drive the same way home, I frequently channel-surf and—" she lifted her hand, palm facing her and gave her fingers a wiggle "—normally paint my nails different colors. Which is why I frustrated you."

You're still frustrating me. "Because I'm so organized."

"Bingo. I try but I can't fight my genes. I am chaos. You are order." She poked her finger at the paper. "This is so you. I should've expected a list."

Finn felt unease prickle the back of his neck at her familiarity. "What about our mutual likes? Dislikes?"

"You liked shoes off in the house. Coats hung on the rack. You loved soccer and socializing. And judging by the time you spent at work, you loved your job. I liked to spend a whole day reading a book, I frequently ignored my closest friends for months and—" she gave a small laugh "—I let my clothes fall wherever I took them off."

Lust exploded as his imagination shot into overdrive, at the thought of her stripping down to her underwear. Something pink and shiny with lace...

"I remember leaving my shoes at the front door once," she elaborated, oblivious to the fine line she trod. "You used it to start an argument about why I should be neater. You nearly broke your neck falling over them," she challenged, lifting her eyebrows.

"Opposites attract," he murmured.

"So they say."

"Any other differences?"

"I liked solitude. You craved company. I was more spontaneous and you were the Planner From Hell. You had a schedule for everything—holidays, work, exercise. It drove me nuts."

"Yet we took off on a backpacking trip."

"Maybe I was rubbing off on you."

"Hard to believe we didn't end up killing each other." He smiled.

Just when he'd finally let himself believe that maybe he had this situation under control, her smile disappeared.

"We'd argue but we always made up." She glanced away as a gentle flush bloomed across her cheeks. "But our marriage was based on a lie. I thought you were someone else—just a regular guy."

"I *am* a regular guy."

"A regular guy," she repeated incredulously. "Right. A workaholic millionaire who featured on the front page of every national paper in Denmark. Who owns a castle and dated supermodels."

"I'll not apologize for my family or the European press, Ally," he growled. "You, more than anyone, know that's not the total of who I am."

I don't know who you are now, Ally thought glumly. Focusing on polishing her cutlery for the third time, she felt his eyes dissect her every move.

Finally she smoothed out the tablecloth and rested her elbows on the top. "So how is your memory supposed to return?"

"Since I'm such a 'special case,' as the doctors say, I'm not entirely sure. The executors have given me until the end of May, so the more time we spend together, the better our chances."

Ally gave an inward groan. Another month, tops, and she'd

be unable to hide her pregnancy any longer. And the more time she spent skipping merrily down memory lane the more her hormones would go haywire.

Of all the dumb things to do, agreeing to this had to take the cake. Adult Ally wanted to get it over quickly, but impulsive Ally ached to touch him, wanted to drag out the moments to see if he still felt as good as he once had when she had the full intimate rights of his wife.

Impulsive Ally—or should that be crazy Ally?—wanted *him*—his warm body, his wild lovemaking, his hot, wet kisses—without giving a single thought to the morning after.

And that scared her because it would be so very easy to give in.

He was interested. The heat behind his eyes was as familiar as his arousal had once been beneath her fingers. A guarded wanting, cultivated from spending his life in the limelight, under public scrutiny. As if he were unsure who was watching but a little unable to control his desire anyway.

Despite the doomed situation, it was still as thrilling to the primitive woman in her now as it was before.

To hide the rising heat in her face—not to mention other parts of her body—Ally refocused on the list of questions, scanning the neatly typed page while her breath returned to normal.

But it hitched again as she went down the list. "Some answers you're not going to like."

His eyebrow kinked up questioningly.

"This one. Did we ever cheat on each other."

Those brows took a dive. "Did you?"

She shook her head, swallowing the stab of hurt. "Not me. You."

Eight

"Are you sure?" he demanded.

Ally nodded sadly.

"Who?"

"One of your Danish friends—the daughter of some count. She had a huge crush on you."

Her reply was cut short with the arrival of their appetizers. As soon as the waitress left, he said, "Go on."

"There's not much more to tell." She picked up her fork and started picking at her avocado salad. "You thought it was flattering. We argued—as always—especially about what you told her when she admitted her attraction."

"What did I say?"

"If I recall correctly, 'If I wasn't married to Ally, things would be different.'"

"I see."

She shook her head. "No, Finn, you didn't see. You didn't

see how this sounded to someone who had feelings for you. It wasn't a gentle letdown. It was a promise. It was like you were just passing time with me and that she could be the next in line after we broke up." She tasted remembrance in her mouth, bitter and sharp. "You were giving her hope, permission to pursue you."

"Wait—did I sleep with her?"

She shook her head and forced her voice low, starkly aware of their public location. "Being unfaithful is more than just physical. If your mind had been on our marriage you would have let her down. But you gave her belief there was a chance. You were furious when I wanted you to cut all contact with her. That—" she swallowed convulsively "—just confirmed you and I were doomed."

Finn opened his mouth to argue but the look on her face had him shutting it.

There was no doubting the barely suppressed hurt shadowing her eyes, the tightness bracketing her mouth. She was telling the truth.

A gentle throb started behind his eyes. The more he discovered about himself, the more he didn't want to know. Was he responsible for destroying their marriage with his selfishness and arrogance?

He remembered his friends exchanging strange looks, their barely hidden alarm when he said or did certain things. It was beginning to take on a whole new meaning.

He'd been forced to take a long hard look at his life, at what made him tick and who he'd become.

I've changed. Whatever I was before, I'm different now.

Confusion bubbled up inside but he forced it down. *Now, here, isn't the place to do this.*

So they ate in silence, until their plates were cleared and the main course was served.

He stared at his food and realized he wasn't that hungry after all.

"How's your steak?" she finally asked.

Finn pushed his plate over. "Try some."

She hesitated, her expression wary, as if he'd offered to strip naked and dance on the table. Then she took her fork and stuck it in a piece of his filet.

Finn watched her slowly slide the shiny prongs between her lips and an almighty shot of lust stabbed him below the belt, bringing his groin to sudden and painful attention.

She chewed slowly. "Mmm, that's good. Here, try mine." She wound her fork around her spaghetti and proffered it.

Riveted, he watched her hand cup under the fork when a strand of pasta unraveled, the way she parted her lips as he took the food in his mouth. The way she gave him a tentative "good, huh?" smile and nodded as he chewed.

And the food could have been sawdust for all the attention he gave it.

"Great." It lodged in his throat, a mass of tastelessness, and he reached for his wine to swill it down. "So," he began, desperate to get back to neutral territory, "tell me about your family."

He knew it was the wrong topic when she glanced away.

"There's nothing much to say. My father's dead, my mother lives her own life. The most important person in my life is my grandma, who is currently on a three-month cruise in the South Pacific. End of mystery."

Hardly. "Tell me more."

"We're here to discover your past, not mine."

He paused to search her face intently. "What are you hiding, Ally?"

She said nothing, just sat back in her seat with a panicked expression.

For one second Finn thought she was going to run. He watched as she shifted uneasily in her chair, her hands tightening convulsively around the arms.

"Nothing."

Then she closed off her expression and focused on her plate with misplaced intensity.

Emotion and duty grappled for top honors until weariness engulfed him, forced him back in the chair. He just wanted him memories back so he could rectify a grave injustice, didn't she understand that? But he also found himself wanting to erase the distress in her eyes. She looked like someone who laughed often, the creases around her eyes and sensual curved lips made just for it. But since he'd arrived he was well aware she had barely managed a smile.

Indecision tugged him in a thousand different directions, sending that familiar ache into the base of his neck.

He opted for safe ground instead. "When did you decide to write full-time?" He felt the fledgling headache ease a fraction.

She glanced up. "So you didn't save my e-mails? No," she amended, shaking her head. "Why would you?"

"There's nothing on my computer."

She nodded sadly and Finn felt his good intentions bite him in the rear. "You sent back our wedding photos, all my letters—"

"Not all of them."

"No," she conceded. "And I'm wondering why."

"And I'd love to tell you. But, you know…" He tapped his head.

Covering her small smile at his black humor, she took a sip of water and rolled it around her tongue as if savoring a particularly good vintage. Finn dragged his gaze away from her mouth. *Since when have I been so fascinated by a woman's mere body movements?*

"I quit my job last week," she said. "I worked at *Bliss* magazine for the past two months, editing, writing in-house articles. I also wrote their book review column."

He leaned in closer, so that all the noise and bustle of the restaurant faded into the background and nothing existed outside her intriguing scent and the masked expression in her eyes.

"What kind of book are you writing?"

"Speculative fiction. Time-travel futuristic," she amended at the blank look in his eyes.

"How long have you been writing?"

"Since I was thirteen."

"Did I ever read any?"

"Once."

"And? Did I like it?"

"You said my heroine was too butch."

He picked up his glass with a grimace. "That was… insensitive of me."

Ally resisted the urge to pinch herself. Her attention went to the generous swell of his mouth as he drew the rim of his glass across his bottom lip and studied her.

The change in him was disturbing her more deeply every minute. If she couldn't rely on Finn's predictability, what *could* she rely on?

"I read that writers don't make much money," he said.

"Not in the beginning. But I'm doing some freelance to compensate. Editing, articles. Since I left my job I haven't been happier."

It was only half true. She was happy she didn't have to see Simon's pretty-boy face again. Happy she could set her own schedule and devote all her time to writing. The downside was, of course, her unhealthy savings. She really needed to see a financial planner but couldn't afford—

"What about the apartment? You said you pay rent," Finn interrupted, her voice of pessimism.

"But I'll soon own it outright. So—" she ignored his dark frown "—getting back to our problem. Tell me what the doctors said."

After a pause he said, "The technical term is post-traumatic amnesia, which results from a head injury."

Ally nodded. "What about retrograde amnesia—the loss of memories of past events?"

"Ruled out when I started remembering." At her quizzical look, he added, "The memory's unlikely to return at all with retrograde."

"You've done your homework."

Finn nodded. "I've read everything on the subject. Even the stuff in the trial stage."

"Have you tried hypnotherapy?"

"*Ja.*"

"Acupuncture?"

"A few times."

"Drugs?"

"No." He reached for the butter and smeared some on his bread roll. "No drugs. Anyway, they're usually used to offset dementia in the elderly. I'm frustrated, *elskat,* not crazy."

Ally toyed with her glass, tracing the stem with a forefinger. His endearment came just as easily to his lips as if he'd never stopped saying it. Yet there was something more sincere in that little word—loosely translated it meant *little love*—than the million times he'd said it before. And because she couldn't help it, thoughts of their near-kiss flooded in, leaving her gasping in a rush of sudden desire and wanting.

As if sensing the direction of her thoughts, he gave her an enquiring smile. "What?"

Desperate to focus on something else, to appear calm

despite her churning insides and pounding heart, she said, "The change in you. It's…" She placed her cutlery together across the plate. "You're different."

"How?"

"You're less restless. More centered. And you seem more empathetic," she explained.

"Is this your way of saying I was an impatient jerk?"

Ally couldn't help but smile at his chagrin.

"No." She pushed her plate aside and folded her arms on the table. "But there was always a part of you I felt I couldn't reach. As though you'd closed yourself off. That part only got bigger once we were in Denmark."

But now… He'd been more open with her in the last day than during the entire time she'd known him. That glaring difference sent a strange feeling of dread shooting through her, as if he expected the same in return.

And that thought scares me.

"What did you see in me?" Finn asked, his expression deadly serious.

"You had this aura—an air of confidence. For someone completely lacking in it, it just…drew me. You were fascinating, in control and wildly attractive." She watched his sensuous mouth curve up. "Don't get too full of yourself. You had a tendency to be way too sure of your charms."

"Was I?"

"Yes. All you had to do was crook your little finger and…"

"And?"

She colored the most attractive shade of pink, Finn thought with amusement.

"You get the picture."

"Maybe you'll have to spell it out," he teased, and was rewarded with a wide-eyed look that made him want to lean over and kiss her. Wouldn't *that* be as surprising as hell?

She blinked. "And you still won't take no for an answer."

"I'm determined."

"I would've gone for stubborn."

"Ouch." He grabbed his chest melodramatically. "You're sharp."

"You'd better believe it."

"And is my face different, too, or is staring one of your strange habits?"

She flushed again, much to his delight. "You're still the most focused person I know. Here—" she dug around in her bag and came up with notepad and a pen "—I'll make a time line."

"A what?"

"A time line. You know, plotting relevant events in date order—"

"I know what a time line is."

"Good. Can you order me a soda?" Ally slapped the notepad down on the table and began scribbling.

She'd finished by the time her drink arrived. She swirled the ice around in the glass and took a long gulp. Instead of being pleased at her efficiency he was glaring at the timeline like he would a cubic zirconia in a diamond lineup.

She tilted the straw at him. "Can't read my handwriting?"

He looked up, transferring his loaded green gaze to her. "Let me get this straight. We met in April last year, left Sydney in May to go traveling. We got married in August then arrived in Denmark in October. Then you left in December, just before the New Year."

"Yep." She took another drink and leaned back in the uncomfortable chair to relieve her backache. In the last half hour, it had upgraded to excruciating, and the sudden reality of her impending pregnancy threw her for a loop. With a sigh she shifted in her seat. "You briefed me just before we touched down in Copenhagen but I knew there was more to it than your

'I've got a bit more money than I let on.'" She gave him an ironic smile. "And then your stepmother called the same day and beat you to the explanation."

"And you believed her?"

"Did she lie to me, Finn? Were you not engaged before you met me? Weren't you being groomed to marry some wealthy woman with a title so your family's assets and status would continue to grow?"

"That was Marlene's grand plan, one both my father and I agreed was ridiculous. Did you even listen to my side of it?"

"That wasn't the point. You didn't trust me enough to tell me before then. Marlene not only hated me for ruining her plans, but she saw me as competition. And to top it off, I was now one of the most talked-about foreigners in the country, my every move scrutinized, dissected and judged. I tried for nearly three months, but I couldn't live like that."

"Not even for me?"

"No," she said flatly. "You get happily-ever-after in fiction. Not in real life."

"I'm not an idiot, Ally. I know relationships have to be nurtured. Cultivated. Worked at." The unspoken accusation hung like an early-morning fog in the air.

What could she say? *I was scared? I was way too young? I didn't want you to hate me because I'd decided to keep our baby?*

"You quit a marriage on one mistake," he said finally.

Unprepared for the blow, she blinked in shock. "You knowingly lied to me!"

"And you couldn't commit."

"*You* couldn't trust."

"How can I defend myself when I can't remember?"

"Oh, and accusing me of being uncommitted is fair?" She crossed her arms.

"You don't know what I'm thinking."

"Now we get to it." She leaned forward to emphasize the point. "Once we set foot in Denmark you closed off as if you were shutting the damned door on me. You were cold and aloof and preoccupied with how your family was handling the attention. You never once asked me how *I* was handling it."

His eyes bored into hers. "You handled it," he said softly, "by running away."

Nine

"**I** will not," Ally said calmly, even though her stomach began to pitch, "apologize for the past, Finn. It's over and done with. You accused me once of giving up—I won't let you do it all over again."

A strained standoff thundered between them as they glared at each other, both unwilling to back down.

As if sensing the tension, the waitress silently brought the bill then slunk off. Ally shifted in her chair again and as Finn reached for the bill, she closed her eyes in respite.

Finn stared at her, a thousand conflicting battles warring inside as his head began to ache. How could he trust her answers when he could see her hesitation, hear the half truths? Yet despite his simmering frustration, she tugged at something in his heart, at a place where her breath, her scent, her skin, felt warm and comforting. A place where small fragmented memories dashed by before he had a chance to grab them, study them and make sense of everything. She felt somehow so familiar but yet a complete stranger.

Control was something he'd been short of since landing in Sydney. Right now he was sitting in the middle of a wild tossing ocean with no rescue in sight.

It has to be tough on her, too. He noticed the bunched-up shoulders, the ramrod-straight back. The tension bracketing her eyes. She looked as tired as he felt.

Regret began to seep in. Without a word he reached over and placed a finger on her forehead to gently rub the frown lines. She jumped as if he'd poked her in the eye.

"Let's go. How much do I owe you?" She scraped back her chair and got to her feet, but when she reached for her bag he stilled her with a hand.

"I'm paying," he said. "That's okay."

She pulled away far too quickly. "I need to give you half."

He shook his head. "This is my problem. I can afford to foot the bill."

Her whole body stiffened. "I'll pay my own way, thanks."

"Why?"

"Because I want to." She stared down at him. "You're already buying my apartment. I don't need you to pay for me, too. I won't be indebted to anyone."

If this works you won't be much longer, lille skat.

She shoved some notes into his hand and turned, marching down the cobbled street. His eyes roamed over her lush curves as he followed her determined walk.

Finn insisted on collecting her box of memories and Ally relented, feeling the stresses of the day bearing down on her.

She unlocked her apartment door, pushed it open and flourished dramatically. "Welcome to chez McKnight."

Finn walked past the small alcove with its coat hooks and

shoe rack, into the large living room painted the dark blue of sky just before sunset. A worn lounge chair in burnt orange dominated the center, facing the TV unit sitting flush on the left wall. On the right was her workspace—a long battered desk complete with computer, printer and scanner. The rest of the space was taken up with floor-to-ceiling shelves. Those shelves not housing books two deep and shoved in any which way, held candle holders, picture frames or other knickknacks Marlene would have sneeringly termed "dust gatherers." Dead ahead, behind white gauzy curtains, was a sliding glass door that opened to a small balcony. To the left, past the TV, lay a door he assumed led to the kitchen, and past that, a hallway.

Framed pictures dotted the walls—album art from what he guessed was a favorite band, a classic Van Gogh café scene. A spectacular shot of Las Vegas at night.

The colors were bold, vibrant and strong. A testament to the woman living there. The whole place felt…comfortable somehow. Like the essence of Ally, her energy and aspirations and haven all rolled into one. He sensed her pride and contentment in this place as if it were the fanciest apartment in Copenhagen.

This isn't a woman who needs money to complete her, his conscience whispered.

Ally locked the door behind her. "I'll go get that box."

When she returned, Finn was scanning her bookshelf. Glancing briefly to her desk then back to him, she wondered whether he'd noticed the finance books she'd left open. But he seemed more interested in her photos than in checking out her workspace.

She placed the plastic box on the coffee table as he scooped up her keys.

"I'll go put it in the car." He picked up the box with

apparent ease. "I don't know how late we'll be so you'd better pack some clothes. You can spend the night."

Four months ago that would've been a demand made in heaven. Not today.

Still, she swallowed her retort and nodded curtly. *Bite the bullet and get it over with. Then you can have your life back.* "I'll be down in a second."

Quickly she went to the bedroom and threw a change of clothes and other necessities into an overnight bag. Just as she was about to pull the door closed behind her, the intercom buzzed.

"Hello?"

"It's Simon. Can I come up?"

The world stopped turning for just one second as her heart forced a raw, angry breath into her throat. "No."

"I need to talk to you about work," he insisted.

"I don't work for you anymore, Simon."

"Look, can we not have this conversation like this? Can I come up?"

"I'm coming down."

She slammed the door and began to descend, but to her surprise she spotted Simon rounding the stairwell.

"I held the door open for some guy with a box." He gave her that look, one that she'd once compared to a little boy's mischievous grin. Now it just made her want to slap him. A dark sinking feeling settled in her stomach.

She crossed her arms protectively. "How did you find me?"

"Personnel files." His thousand-watt smile was meant to be persuasive, seductive. It left her cold. As did his top-to-toe inspection that felt cheap and nasty. "You're looking great. How are you?"

"Still pregnant." His cocky smile dropped quicker than a shooting star, Ally noted with satisfaction. "What do you want?"

"Ally. Do you really want to talk about this—" he waved an all-encompassing hand with only a mild look of disdain "—in this hallway?"

She gave a snort. She didn't want this man in her personal, private space. Eyeing her reading material, slouching on her furniture. Tainting her sanctuary.

"Say what you have to and leave."

With a sigh, he leaned against the balustrade, his arm draped casually along the railing. She couldn't help but compare his expensive I'm-someone-very-important-and-very-hip look to Finn's overt masculinity. And she found Simon's desperate need for wealth and show a pale comparison to her husband's aura of power and confidence.

"Max sent me," he said.

Ally frowned. "Why?" She didn't think the editor-in-chief even knew her name.

"It's about the *Bliss* Awards."

"The press office deals with that."

"You're getting one next week and Max wants you there to accept it."

Ally's mouth sagged open for one second before she realized and snapped it shut.

Simon continued somewhat smugly. "Your column had the highest reader rating since...well—" he shrugged "—since we started a book column. Max isn't happy that you left or that no one wants to do your job. He wants you to come back."

"I'm getting a *Bliss* Award." Through the haze of incredulity, Ally failed to notice Simon crowding her space. It was the strong whiff of oriental musk that hit her like a speeding reality check, sending her backward a step.

Simon either didn't notice or chose to ignore it.

"Yeah. Favorite Column or something. Ally. We have to talk about you. Us." He reached out and stroked her arm, but she quickly pulled away. He suppressed a frown. "I know you've been a little…emotional since we… Since you and I… Well, let's forget about that scene in my office and start over."

She rounded her eyes. "Oh, how generous of you."

"Look. The thing is, Max wants you back. And—" he brushed an imaginary piece of lint off his arm "—people have been talking."

"About?"

He flicked his dismissive brown-eyed gaze down to her stomach then up again. "Us."

The jerk couldn't even say the word. "So?"

"People think we had sex."

She gave a short laugh. "Wasn't that the whole point of New Year's Eve? So you could boast about it afterwards?"

"Ally. Hon. Calm down."

"And we can't have me getting too emotional, can we? I might go and do something completely stupid."

He looked alarmed. "You wouldn't…say anything, would you?"

"Take your hand off my arm."

He withdrew and she took the opportunity to start down the stairs. *The jerk. No, the mega jerk.* She threw him a furious glance as he followed her, deliberately letting him dangle. "Who knows? I'm in such a delicate, emotional state I'm likely to do anything."

"Look, Ally," he cajoled, the smooth inflection in his voice getting her back up "We should discuss this. You can have your job back. You'd like that, right?"

"No. I wouldn't." Now that she had him panicky, the victory seemed all too ironic. "Save it, Simon. I've got to go."

"Can we negotiate?"

"You've got nothing I want," she stumbled on a step and gasped, grabbing the railing. Abruptly she slowed her pace.

Behind her, she caught the waves of irritation rolling off him, his frustrated stomp as he was forced to follow her down the stairs.

"What is your problem?" Simon muttered.

"Well, it was you. But not anymore."

"You'd miss out on an important night in your career and a well-paid job because of a misunderstanding between us?"

When she remained silent he grabbed her arm and yanked her to a stop. She winced. "You haven't answered me."

"Let my wife go."

They both whirled. Finn was standing two steps down with fury barely restrained in his expression. His regal, stiff bearing emphasized the unspoken menace reverberating around him like dark thunderclouds.

Simon's hand dropped.

"Wife?" He glared accusingly at Ally. "Since when have you been married?"

"That's none of your business." She shot Finn a meaningful look and said quietly, "I'd like some privacy."

Finn frowned, eyes full of watchful intensity as he kept them pinned on Simon. "No."

"That wasn't a question."

"I will not leave you alone with him."

"Finn—"

"Ally. He touched you and I do not like it."

"Don't interfere," she hissed.

He finally transferred his attention from Simon to her and his gaze became a shade colder. "I can't promise that."

"Then I've got nothing to say," she walked down the steps, brushed past Finn and stalked out to the car.

"Don't be stupid, Ally!" Simon called across the car park as Finn followed her. "I'm offering you a job. And we both know the Awards could be a deal-maker for you. When will you get another chance?"

"I'm driving," Finn commanded as she approached the driver's side. With a glare, she rounded the front and yanked open the passenger door.

Finn started the engine and pulled out of the car park. She watched Simon's impeccably suited form disappear when they turned the corner.

"Idiot," she muttered under her breath. "Conceited, self-important, pain-in-the—"

"Who was that?" Finn asked.

"My ex-boss."

"He offered you your job back."

"Yes."

"What else?"

"That's none of your—"

"If you tell me the truth then I won't be forced to jump to conclusions," Finn said calmly.

"Fine. I'm getting a *Bliss* Award." At his blank look, she explained, "The magazine hands out awards to its best writers, as voted by the readers. It's *the* most-talked-about night of the year amongst the magazine publishers, a red-carpet affair with an A-list a mile long. You get free food, booze and top Aussie bands at the afterparty. It's on every staff writer's wish list."

The tight muscles in her neck eased as the implication began to sink in. "Getting an invite alone would warrant high-end bids. But to actually receive an award…"

"It's like being a geek and getting told you're invited to the cool kids' party."

"Yes." *A Bliss Award! Me!* Despite her feelings about the messenger, pride teased her mouth into a small smile. "The editor-in-chief has asked for me personally. And if I'm not there…"

Simon will be in bi-i-i-g trouble, she thought devilishly.

"When?" Finn asked.

"Next Saturday."

"I'll take you," he said firmly.

"No, you won't."

"It's a partnered function, right?"

"Yes, but—"

"So I'll take you."

"No."

"Yes."

"No, you won't."

"Yes, I will. Look—" he paused, his brows stubbornly set in a frown "—I'm not going to play this yes-and-no game with you."

"Then don't. Cinderella is perfectly capable of taking herself to the ball." She glared at him as they stopped at a red light. "If I were going—which I'm not." *Think of all the money you'd save by not buying a new dress. Or shoes.*

He gave her a long deliberate look, as if he was torn between throttling her and kissing her. Her skin prickled with the thrill of uncertainty.

The moment shattered when the lights changed. He eased his foot off the brake and refocused on the road.

"Why aren't you going?"

"Maybe I want to see Simon get chewed out—or worse— by the boss."

"Ally."

"Oh, all right. Because—" she hesitated "—Simon tried to… He wanted us to be more than boss and employee. I said no."

In the sudden silence, the air inside the car slowly filled with hot tension. "Did he hurt you?"

"No."

"Did you quit or were you fired?"

She sighed.

"Tell me."

"I quit."

"So you let him get away with it?"

She flushed. File a formal complaint because she was lacking in judgment and starved for physical contact? She could see the headlines now: Pregnant Unemployed Local Sues Boss and Dies of Embarrassment.

"I hated that job anyway," she muttered.

"So you'd miss out on a night you've worked towards your whole life because your boss was a pig."

"Well, put like that... Yeah."

"I thought you had more backbone than that, *lille skat.*"

She refused to voice her real doubts aloud. That if she and Finn started acting like a couple in public, then maybe she'd start thinking they were. And that could never, ever happen.

They drew to a stop as the traffic banked up.

"But I guess that's your choice," he commented casually, eyes fixed firmly on the road. "You could, of course, dictate the terms of your return if they want you back that badly. But if you're not going to the awards, what's the point? You obviously didn't like the job."

"I loved the job," she scowled, completely aware of her denial only moments before.

"So you're a coward."

"I'm not!"

"Seems to me," he continued, ignoring the fury in her eyes, "that you're afraid that people will be talking about you. And if I go, they'll be talking about us."

"That's not—"

"It could help with my memory."

"How?"

"Us, together. At a formal function. We *did* go to those sometimes?"

"A few black ties in Denmark," she grudgingly admitted. "But you're drawing a long bow here."

"A what?"

"Jumping to wild conclusions."

"Maybe," he said. "But again, it's your choice. We'll just have to spend more time together in other ways."

She gritted her teeth as the traffic resumed its crawl. She knew what he was doing, but dammit, the logic in his argument made sense.

"Ally? Can I come?"

She blinked, feeling the heat spread up from belly to face. The new Finn, the concerned, almost jealous man beneath the controlled exterior, baffled her. And when he shot her a scorching look that stretched the seams of her shredded control…

"You may get recognized."

He shrugged. "I doubt it."

"It's black tie."

"I'll buy something."

"You won't know anyone."

"I like meeting new people."

"These things can run on for hours."

"Do I have another place to go?"

"People will think we're *together*."

She caught his look of… She frowned. Disappointment? Surely not. "Is even the thought of people thinking we're a couple that repugnant to you?"

She felt her face heat up again, this time from embarrassment. "No."

"Then, Ally, *lille skat*—" the endearment brushed her like a gentle kiss "—let me come. I want to come. With you."

She squirmed and was thankful when the traffic began to move again. "Will you stop saying that word?"

"What word?" he murmured.

"Come."

"What's wrong with *come?*" If a man could purr, he'd be doing it now.

"You know what it means in English," she retorted, her face still burning.

It was no help at all to catch that roguish look, his eyes crinkling and the dimple that flashed as he quickly feigned innocence. "Ah, Ally, I didn't know you were such a—"

"Prude?"

"Innocent," he amended, laughter still in his eyes.

"Well, now you know. Again. I embarrass easily. Remember that."

"Oh, I will."

Ten

"So that's everything," Ally said, leaning back into the couch with a sigh. They'd sorted all the papers in her box into chronological order, from the first card to the last damning e-mail. Every teasing word, every sexual innuendo. It was Ally stripped down to her most bare, her most vulnerable. Finn felt like a hijacked passenger along for an emotional ride, experiencing the highs of her optimistic musings, the very lows of her doubts.

And yet he couldn't remember any of it.

He'd felt her nervousness and embarrassment when he'd been reading the most intimate of notes. She'd fidgeted, got up to get drinks, even wandered off onto the balcony for a good fifteen minutes. And still the result was the same.

They both sat there, staring at the neat piles of paper in silence, until she broke it with another small sigh and said again, "So that's it."

"There's nothing else?" he asked unnecessarily. She shook her head.

"So how do you—?"

"I don't know," he snapped.

She pulled back, hurt reflecting in her eyes. Immediately he regretted it.

"Maybe," he continued more calmly, "we need a break. I'll order dinner."

She nodded. "I'll take a shower."

He rubbed his temple with a frustrated grunt but jumped when he felt her hand go to his shoulder.

"We'll get there, Finn," she said softly. Before he could answer, she withdrew and was on her feet.

Damn, damn, damn.

Half truths, fractured memories and wild conclusions all fought against the confusion in his mind. He knew the future of his family legacy was at stake. Yet his simple desire to know what had happened to him and Ally was gaining more momentum. He needed to understand just who he had been, so he could finally figure out the person he had finally become.

Why did he let his wife leave? Why didn't he jump on a plane and bring her back home?

It was one of a million questions that remained unanswered.

He balled his fist in frustration and rubbed his temple, the ever-present ache behind his eyes steadily growing.

The part of him that had been cut by Marlene's betrayal and scorched by a blank memory was enough to keep his guard up. Yet the impression he got from Ally, his quickly forming opinion, was nothing he could have prepared for. Yes, there were still some things she hadn't elaborated on. But she had also been brutally and disturbingly honest and for that, he was grateful.

He'd considered telling Ally about his father's bequest

then offering to buy her out. And for every reason why, he came up with one big why not. What if his memory didn't return? To give her that kind of expectation, that dream, then pull the carpet from under her when it failed to come to fruition, would be unforgivable.

Failing the company is a possibility, but not until after I'm satisfied I've done everything I can. I can live with that. But I cannot live with failing Ally again.

Dangling that kind of carrot under her nose then yanking it away sounded like something his former self would have contemplated. But not now. Silence was detrimental until his memory returned.

He eased back onto the couch, rubbing his chin. His head felt as if it were being pulled in ten different directions. His skin tingled as though it were stretched taut to the bone, skin he'd been itching on and off for the last hour. The phone call home had only confirmed time was running out. Marlene was making threats again, the Board of Directors was wavering and the estate executors had warned that they must start drafting up proceedings in case his mission failed.

He sighed, leaned forward and picked up a card. The front depicted a black cartoon cat in a crowd full of white cats. He opened it up and the simple words *I miss you* struck him square in the chest.

Ally was a woman he was intensely turned on by, that he knew. His body had been in a constant state of arousal, yet he was troubled by that one half truth in the restaurant as much as he was stirred by her curvy lushness.

He threw the card on the table and reached for his coffee.

In the silent air of night, their near-kiss, the incredible, intense burst of heat and lust that had gotten so completely out of control, began to play with his mind. Despite her thin attempts at keeping a cool facade, Ally didn't respond like a woman in control of anything. Her expression, the look on her face had been as far from control as he could imagine. He imagined her lips, her teeth, her tongue. And her hands, touching him, flaming his skin, making him want to throw her to the floor and ravish her until the pressures of his former life were a distant memory.

His wife was definitely turned on to the promise of any physical contact.

Many of his friends had admitted they thought his marriage was his way of getting back at Marlene for practically throwing all those hand-picked women at him. But dragging Ally into a family feud just so he could annoy his stepmother? His common sense revolted at the childish idea. There were a lot of things he'd learnt of his past self that felt…wrong, somehow. And right now, he didn't know what to think, especially with his body chiming into the debate and screwing with his mission.

He rose, went over to the patio door and yanked it open, then took a deep breath as he stepped outside, his lungs filling with fresh sea air. The ocean immediately calmed him, as if it stirred more pleasant memories.

Finn folded his arms on the balcony and stared out over the pitch-black ocean. A gentle breeze whipped across his skin, bringing with it the smell of rain and an outdoor barbecue from the Coogee Bay Hotel on the corner. He heard a bird's *ack-ack* night call, then the rowdy echo of song from a couple of drunken revelers.

In dazed exasperation he tried to make sense of what had happened so far. Ally's walls of preservation—understandable given his past record. His attraction—simply physical.

Her push-pull response to him…confusing.

What does that have to do with getting your memory back?

Yet their almost-kiss that morning and the consequences

it provoked stuck in his head and rolled around until something finally clicked.

The first time his memory had tweaked, he'd been reading her letters, breath quickening as his past had unfolded between those pages. The second time she'd been within kissing distance and again, the familiar up-tempo heartbeat, the rush of memories echoing in his head.

Conclusion?

The answer was so simple he gave a shout of surprise. He'd been so determined to reason away, fight or ignore this attraction that he hadn't realized…

Rejuvenated with purpose, he turned on his heel and stalked into the lounge room then down the hall, intent on organizing his plan with an icy shower. He was yanking open the bathroom door before realizing his folly.

His wife, her wet silhouette, was on display past the clear glass shower door.

He closed his mouth so quickly his teeth clicked. Slowly, he ran his eyes down the curve of her back, following the direction of the streaming water over honeyed skin. The gentle, intensely erotic curve of her bottom, those shapely thighs and strong, defined calves.

His mouth went dry at the sight.

She was his. He had touched, kissed and explored every inch of that skin. Possessed her body and her love.

He could yank open that door and take her with the water pounding down on them both, fueling the simmering tension that was just below the surface.

His body ached for her, the rush of blood pounding to his groin, desperate, urgent.

Her gentle humming snapped him back to reality. With a shuddering breath he turned away, into the alcove that housed the sink, and yanked on the faucet. After splashing cold water on his face he looked up, dripping, staring in the mirror—pale, dark-circled eyes, in need of a shave. Ally might not like what he was about to suggest—hell, she might even refuse point-blank—but he had to take a shot.

With a last lingering glance at her reflection in the mirror, he retreated, gently closing the bathroom door behind him.

When Ally emerged dressed in a robe, her hair turbaned in a towel, Finn was silently waiting in the living room.

"Well." She gave him a tentative smile, but his face remained impassive. "That bathroom was amazing. Are you…"

He was in her personal space quicker than a heartbeat. She backed up against the wall until she could go no farther. His body pressed up then settled against hers, the heavy robe ruffling a sigh with the friction. His hands went to her shoulders, his face close…too close.

"Ever since I saw you, I've been wondering what you'd taste like."

Through her shock, she could see the tension in his jaw, the purpose in his green eyes. He wasn't happy about that rough confession.

And then, against all reason, against every promise he'd made, Finn kissed her.

Eleven

The kiss was pure Finn, everything Ally remembered, his smell, his skin, his lips. They took, they devoured. For one heartbreaking second, time actually *did* stand still, throwing her common sense into chaos and tumbling her memory back to when she'd been in love with this hypnotic man.

Danger danced across her skin as his smell, all spicy and male, stormed her defenses like an invading Viking army of centuries past. She felt his body against hers harden, the honed muscle settling into unyielding granite.

Yet beneath his uncompromising body, heat radiated out as though it wanted to claim her in its flame. She seesawed between desire and panic, until desire won out.

God forgive me for being weak, but I can't help myself.

With a small whimper, she opened her mouth and invited his tongue in. The small question of doubt flashed into her brain but she ignored it. This moment, this mind-numbing kiss, was hungry and intense and everything she'd missed. Everything in her dreams. So she threw caution to the wind and let herself go.

Finn held her face steady between his hands and took her mouth as if she was his own private banquet. He feasted upon her, tongues tangling, lips crushing, until they were both breathless. He seized everything she offered, not caring that his blood was pounding through his veins so quick and hard that his whole body vibrated with the force of his desire. Not caring that he was here for one purpose only and that didn't include seducing his wife.

Not caring that his knee was wedged between her legs, shoving apart the robe so he could now feel her damp heat of arousal on his thigh.

All it did was serve as fuel to a naked flame, licking him from head to feet. Her towel fell to the floor. He grabbed her nape and with it, handfuls of silky damp hair. Angling her mouth across his and deepening the kiss, he heard her muffled groan of pleasure.

Every nerve exploded, sending shards of pleasure throbbing through his body. His groin pulsed and suddenly he wanted to throw her down onto the floor and bare her body to his gaze. To lick and nibble and taste. To take her every which way he possibly could—from the back, the side, bent over the desk—

The ferocity of his thoughts pulled him up short, dragged his mouth from her swollen one with an oath. Stunned gray eyes stared back at him.

As quickly as Ally had been thrust into the past, reality came crashing back. They were in his hotel room. She was practically naked. His knee was intimately jammed between her legs.

And she was damp with wanting.

That's the way it was, had always been, for her. As if she

was a Christmas tree festooned with lights and with one flick of the switch, Finn could turn her on.

Her readiness for sex had become just one of their many intimate jokes.

His thigh tensed and moved, steely muscle rubbing damp wetness. With a small groan of dismay she pulled away, then winced as his hands remained entangled in her hair.

"You promised!" She jerked back, desperate to put some distance between her memories and the overwhelming reality of the here and now.

He finally released her, dragging his fingers through her hair slowly, almost longingly. As if he'd been wondering what she felt like and now couldn't get enough of it.

His eyes were dark and filled with passion, his mouth grim. And he had touched things that hadn't been touched in an eternity.

Ally let her arousal dissolve into anger as she took a step back. "Are you trying to seduce me?"

"Can't you feel it?"

Stunned into silence, she shook her head to clear the fuzziness. "What?"

"My theory."

"Your..?"

"Earlier today. After I touched you—"

She flushed. "Yes."

"I was…thinking about your mouth."

She blinked slowly.

Finn felt his throat become thick with the thought of recall, as though he'd swallowed a cup of rich chocolate and couldn't quite clear his voice. With the devil on his shoulder he added with a tilt to his lips, "I was thinking about your lips. Tongue. How you'd smell, all warm and sweaty under me."

She flushed bright red. "And your point is?"

"I remembered something. Which leads me to my theory."

He waited for her to make the connection and when she did, it widened her eyes and sent a flush across her cheeks.

"You think," she said hoarsely, "the key to recovering your memory is you and me…us…?"

"That's exactly what I'm suggesting."

The air was suddenly charged with heat as he watched her shove her hands in her hair, hot-pink nails diving into the tangled mass of damp sun-kissed chestnut. Even something as innocuous as her ears were perfectly shaped, he realized. *Imagine taking that delicate lobe between your teeth and sucking, making her moan with pleasure….*

He felt himself tighten. She was damn cute when she frowned, that little crease of concentration between her eyes so adorable he wanted to kiss it.

"Let me get this straight," she said. "You think us getting physical may result in jogging your memory?"

"Ja."

"How physical?"

He shrugged. "I don't know."

"Is this your way of asking for sex?"

The outrage in her eyes belied her nervousness; she swallowed so hard he could see the muscles convulse in her throat. "Is that the real reason behind this outrageous suggestion? So you can have the convenience of—"

"No," he cut her off firmly. "I don't play games like that. All I know is that yesterday I got a flashback. That's two if you count the time I found your letters in my basement. I think it's somehow caused by intense emotion. Physical emotion. It's a kind of trigger. It must be." He wanted to believe that. *Needed* to believe that.

After seconds of silence, she shook her head.

"How convenient for you." Her eyes blazed at him, sending

a small ribbon of doubt through his mind. "No-strings-attached sex into the bargain. I'll not satisfy an itch you have nor will I let you justify it by dressing it up as a fishing expedition. It's absurd."

"Is it? Are you saying this attraction we have is just a pretense? That I'm faking it? That you are?" His lip curled. "Give me a little credit, Ally. I'm not happy about it. But it doesn't change the fact that it exists. And if we can use it, then all the better."

Her mouth opened—to deny, he thought—but no sound came out. He must have struck a nerve because she snapped her mouth shut and crossed her arms. The light of battle in her eyes dimmed a little.

"No."

"No, what? That you can't feel the attraction?"

"No, I will not have sex with you."

"Are you afraid?"

"Of you? No."

He leaned forward, indulging his senses in the subtle fragrance of her washed hair and clean skin. His blood began to pound. Need clawed at him but he refused to acknowledge the underlying danger beneath it. He would have her, before he drove himself insane imagining what he could not remember. "So why wouldn't it work? Nothing else has come close."

"We've only been at this a day. Shouldn't you give conventional methods a chance before we start jumping into bed?"

"Time is one thing we do not have. It could work."

"And if it doesn't, at least we'd have a good time trying? Don't answer that," she added as he opened his mouth.

He frowned. For a smart woman, she could be incredibly slow on the uptake. They both felt the attraction, the zing between them. They would be great together.

Her eyes squeezed shut as she reached up to shove her hair away again, muttering, "I don't…"

Ally jumped as his hands imprisoned her arms above her head. His body blocked out the light from the small table lamp, cast his face in shadows. Still, she could feel the palpable emotions—irritation, reluctant control and white-hot desire—and she stilled, holding her breath. The way he made her feel so…tiny, so delicate, had once excited her. Now she was just plain aggravated. And hot, which she couldn't blame on the weather. *Rats*.

He ran his gaze over every inch of her face, a silent quest that pulsed with energy. An unexpected image of him taking her here, now, with the elegant velvet-clad walls rubbing against her naked skin stuttered her breath.

She prayed he couldn't sense that. He had always been able to tell when she was aroused; it was as if the man had a high-frequency radar tuned on to her or something.

"We've shared our bodies before," he murmured. "I've touched you intimately. Yet when I get in your personal space or want to know something more than you're prepared to give, you backpedal like a world champion." His unrelenting scrutiny held the power to burn and she could feel her skin begin to sizzle. "What scares you more…bringing up the past? Or the fact that we can't fight this?"

It was a fake kiss, one made just to prove a point. It was hot and powerful and full of pure brute force. His mouth ground down on hers, taking, ravishing without a thought as to what she wanted.

Do something, Finn silently demanded, meeting her furious gaze with his determined one. *Say something. Push me away, so I'll know you don't want this, that you're not interested. Then I'll back off.* But despite the depth of his frustration fuelling the moment, she willingly opened up, wrapped her arms around his neck and sweetly invited his tongue in. It was as if by giving in to him, taking all he had to offer, she could make the moment hers.

The second he realized what she was doing—that she was actually *welcoming* him—he tore his mouth away with a muttered curse.

They stayed stock-still, their racing breaths muting the white noise of their heartbeats. Finn just stared at her, an indefinable expression in his eyes and the restraint of a thousand men holding him in check.

Their weighted silence broke when a car horn tooted below and someone yelled an obscenity.

With her skin tingling with awareness, Ally gently exhaled, gathering enough courage to ensure her voice never wavered.

"I'm not—" She coughed then to clear the passion-laden huskiness. "I'm not scared. You've just changed so much... You're a different person."

He stepped back, giving her a much-needed respite. "So you can't predict how I'll react."

"Exactly."

"I thought I was the one who liked predictability."

"You're twisting my words."

"Am I?"

"Yes. I like my life free of conflict."

His mouth quirked in sudden understanding. "You're conflicted?"

"It's you. You're...you...throw me off balance."

Her eyes widened as he leaned forward to brush away an errant curl from her cheek, gently tucking it behind her ear. Before she had a chance to throw up her shields, he brought his mouth to her ear.

"You're dealing with this the wrong way, Ally. Stop

fighting and it gets easier," he whispered, sending teasing warmth skittering down her back. "And you promised to help me. I intend to see you honor that promise."

Ally wanted to fight against this sexual pull, but ever since he'd turned up, she'd been swimming against the tide. He could be right. And even if he wasn't, her hormonal body wanted this more than anything she'd ever wanted in her entire life. It was stupid to deny it when they were just so physically in tune. And here was the perfect excuse. She could take advantage of her needs with a clear conscience.

What if it works?

With a deep breath she gritted her teeth and shrugged off the delicious anticipation. "No. It's dumb idea." As his mouth quirked, she stammered, "Anyway…we haven't exhausted all other angles yet. There's a way to go yet."

He tilted one eyebrow devilishly. "As you wish. But I don't know why you're fighting it, *elskat*. We have chemistry. Why are you denying the inevitable?"

Twelve

The next morning, as the sun began to rise, Finn gave up all pretense of sleeping and headed for a long, cold shower.

When he padded into the living area, Ally was seated in a corner of the two-seater, legs encased in a pair of cargo pants and curled beneath her, sipping a glass of orange juice.

She'd scraped her hair back into a messy ponytail and the tank strap under her white shirt was slipping off her shoulder. He resisted the sudden urge to straighten that strap, test the warm-looking skin beneath it.

"How did I get to the spare room?" she said, looking up.

"I carried you. You fell asleep on the couch at 1:00 a.m." His smug glance said "I told you so" so clearly she wanted to throw a cushion at him but wisely refrained.

"So you slept well?" he queried. Still damp from the shower, he pulled a towel from his neck and began drying his hair, ignoring her widened eyes.

"Yes, thank you." The small shadows under her eyes belied that, but Finn let it go. "I've been thinking about what you said about the *Bliss* Awards."

"Which part?"

"About it being an important milestone in my career. If I don't turn up it's my loss. If I do, I'm still drawing attention to myself. Either way I lose."

"You don't like the attention?" he asked curiously.

"No. I'm a private person. But if I go, I can use it to my advantage."

"So we're going."

"You don't have to—"

He sighed. "We have no choice. Do you think Simon has kept his mouth shut about me?"

She looked pained. "Probably not. Do you still want to go?"

The inflected doubt in her voice sent a ribbon of protectiveness coursing through him. "I do."

"So we need to get you something formal."

His hands went to the towel to retie it and her eyes followed his movement.

He hid a smile as he ran a hand over rock-hard abs, flicking away the last drops of water. He watched her watch him, her gaze darting up to his. When he winked at her, she looked away, a flush staining her cheeks.

She stared at the mess on the coffee table. "How did you get on with those letters?"

"No improvement in the memory. Yet."

"Oh."

They both fell into significant silence.

"Look," Finn began, his hands on his hips, hating what he was about to say after all that effort to convince them both last night. "If you want to reconsider what I said last night—"

"Do you?"

His blood began to throb again, much to his exasperation. "No."

"Okay." He heard her small intake of breath, as if she were drawing in courage. "So at least I know where you stand. Hopefully, this week might yield better results, especially with these awards. So…" She paused, looking at him expectantly. He just quirked up an eyebrow. Finally she said, exasperated, "go and put something on!"

He smiled again, enjoying her discomfort. "You have a problem with naked?"

"You're not naked. Not completely." She flushed and his grin turned wicked.

"You can always come and watch."

Ally was on her feet quicker than a cat. "I need some air."

Finn smothered a laugh as he went into the master bedroom. *Deny it,* lille skat, *but you are interested.*

He took that as a good sign.

"Are you okay?"

"Will you stop asking me that?" Ally said as they stepped out of another air-conditioned department store and into the afternoon heat of Pitt Street Mall. "I'm fine."

"A woman who tries on a dozen dresses and still walks out empty-handed is not okay."

"I've got a perfectly good outfit at home."

"So you didn't like that blue dress?"

She sighed, remembering the long, flattering empire lines, the satin-ribboned straps. The fashionable jagged hem overlaid with sheer organza that shimmered rainbow colors when she'd moved. "I loved the dress. But I don't need it."

"You still don't look fine."

"Gee, thanks. What are you doing?" She took a step back as he placed a hand on her forehead.

"You're hot."

"It's a hot day."

Ally jammed on her sunglasses as the mall's lunchtime crowd ebbed and flowed around them. The street canopies gave some relief from the sun, but she still felt the trickle of sweat down her back. The warmth under her armpits and the heaviness in the pit of her stomach just made her feel icky—despite all the water she'd drunk and the decent breakfast she'd consumed.

"You look awful." Finn studied her carefully.

"Ever the flatterer." Yet she didn't argue when Finn took her keys as they reached the car, instead gratefully settling in the passenger seat with a sigh.

She must have dozed off because the next thing she knew, Finn was unsnapping her seatbelt, then swinging her up into his arms.

She struggled but he tightened his grip. "Quit it, Ally. I don't want to drop you."

In a sleepy haze she let him carry her up the stairs, open her apartment door with absurd dexterity and finally walk into her bedroom.

But when he deposited her on the bed and began to undo her pants, she shoved him away. "I don't need you to undress me."

He stepped back, crossed his arms and watched her fiddle with the button fly for long agonizing seconds.

"Oh, *for helve*," he muttered, then reached down and flicked open the buttons with ridiculous efficiency. Before she had another chance to protest, he yanked off her pants, pulled the sheet up and placed an impersonal kiss on her forehead.

"Pushy Dane," she muttered, then turned over, shoved a pillow under her head and promptly fell asleep.

Two hours later Ally woke to the annoying jangle of the phone. She let the machine take it, eying the clock: 4:02 p.m.

"Ally? It's Julia."

With a groan, she rolled out of bed. She'd been avoiding her mother's calls since she'd quit the magazine. Telling her would only lead to other things and she just wasn't up to having that you're-going-to-be-a-grandma conversation. Not now. Not yet. Julia's reaction would be typically over the top: enthusiastic and smothering…everything she hated and refused to accept now she was an adult.

Ally snorted as she walked down the hall and into the living room. Grandma Lexie had been her real mother. She'd been there through chicken pox, training bras and first dates. Through career changes, rent increases, bad haircuts and that weird protein diet that had sent her metabolism haywire. And most of all, she'd been a grounded, sympathetic shoulder to cry on when Julia occasionally breezed in with gifts and promises of playing a more permanent role in her life, then inevitably walked right out again.

After she went into the living room and spotted Finn on the balcony, she pressed the playback button on her machine. The first message was from Tony, the following two were hang-ups. The next was her mother.

With an exasperated sigh, she shoved her hair off her forehead.

Finn was on his cell phone, barking out orders in Danish. Then he saw her, said something into the phone and hung up.

"Hey, sleepyhead."

"Hi."

"Come here."

"Why?"

He sighed. "Just do it, Ally."

She took a step forward but it wasn't quick enough. Suddenly he was there, cupping a gentle hand to the nape of her neck and tilting her head forward, massaging her tension with long, expert fingers. The familiar possessiveness made her shiver.

The beep and click of the answering machine echoed in the background. The increasing frustration in her mother's voice as she left yet another message.

Ally closed her eyes and shut it all out, letting Finn's fingers ease the stress and worry away, allowing herself a moment of respite to melt into him, to let her throbbing breasts rest against the heat of his chest and his warm breath feather in her ear…

"Pick up. It's Simon. We need to talk."

Ally sprang back on the end of a shocked gasp.

With a dreadful sense of premonition, she did the only thing she could think of. She ran.

Bad idea. As she turned, the rug bunched under her feet and she lost balance. Finn grabbed her to cushion the fall and they crashed to the floor, both sprawling while the rest of Simon's message reverberated through the room.

"Look, you got me the other day. I thought by springing the Awards on you, you'd have no choice but to say yes. But the thing is, Max is busting my ass to get you there. You know what he's like. So call PR and I'll have two tickets waiting for you. Oh, and you don't need to worry about any awkward moments—I've made other plans for that night."

She closed her eyes and breathed an inward sigh of relief. *Not as bad as I thought.*

Finn's breath stuttered in his throat and hotly grazed her cheek.

"Ally?"

"What?" She strained away, a hard thing to do when he was lying on top of her, her body singing with anticipation at the contact.

"Look at me."

Reluctantly she opened her eyes. Those green depths held a complexity of emotion. Wonder. Surprise. And white-hot desire.

Fear coursed through her veins.

Don't let his touch fool you. But her heart was pounding so heavily she found it hard to breathe.

You're still in love with your husband.

She was shocked, but only for a second. She *did* love him, in ways she'd never realized possible when they had been together. It called to mind the chorus of an old, well-loved song— "I loved you more than I did when you were mine."

She just had to keep reminding herself that he hadn't been hers in a long time. Even though her body still wanted him, she'd thought her head was immune after all they had been through.

She turned her face to the side, as if protecting her thoughts from his probing gaze. "You're crushing me," she finally got out.

When he didn't move, she gently pushed her hands between them. "Finn. Please. I need to get up."

Without a word, he got to his feet, then offered a hand to her.

She took it, absurdly grateful for any physical contact. And without a word, he led her to the couch.

"What are you…?"

"Shhhh, *elskat*. For once let's not say anything."

He kissed her with such passion, such possessiveness that an unbidden glimmer of hope bloomed in the corner of Ally's heart. What if…?

He skimmed his palm over her shoulders to lie possessively against the wild pulse at the base of her neck.

"I'm moving in."

She gaped for one second, until Finn calmly closed her mouth with one finger under her chin.

"Why?" she spluttered.

"You obviously didn't like last night's theory and time is not something we have a lot of. What—you have another suggestion?" he challenged at the look in her eyes.

Nothing that doesn't involve smacking you on the side of the head. "I don't—"

"And I don't give a… What's the word? A *stuff*. That's right. I don't give a *stuff* what you want right now, Ally. We have less than two months to find that codicil. We can't do this by half measures. Or…we could always…"

Ally swallowed thickly as he let that suggestion hang, his eyes focused on her lips. She couldn't stop her plummeting heart every time he mentioned that codicil. It just reinforced the cold, hard truth of his return.

"So I don't have a say in this?" she said softly.

"You could've said no at the start."

"How could I? You practically blackmailed me into it."

A bare hint of surprise and irritation sparked in his green eyes. "*Ja*. And I'm sorry for that." He rubbed his chin with his palm. "I'm just trying to handle this situation as quickly as I can."

A bittersweet emotion sent a pang through her chest, making it hard to breathe.

And right then and there, she wanted more than anything to kick sensible Ally to the curb. To ignore her nagging doubts, the endless what-ifs that the future would bring. Even the heartache that would follow as surely as Finn's departure.

When would she get another chance to enjoy her time with him? If she looked inside her heart and was completely honest, wasn't this something she'd wanted ever since he'd made that midnight call? Yes, she'd have to deal with his leaving eventually, but memories of this time—*their* time— would sustain her through the lonely months and years ahead.

Because there was no way she'd settle for second best. If she couldn't have this man she didn't want any man.

She shrugged and put her hands on her hips, avoiding his eyes. "Fine. You can move in. The quicker we do this, the quicker you can go home."

Thirteen

After a day of so much togetherness, Ally anticipated the coming evening with dark dread. So she wasted time in her bathroom, indulging in a mini facial before stepping into the shower for a long soak. Finally, after pulling on the oldest, rattiest pajamas she could find, she walked into the living room to discover Finn deeply engrossed in the contents of her box.

With everything spread across the coffee table, he was intent on reading a letter. A lock of dusty-blond hair framed the small furrows on his brow and for one heart-pumping second she felt the heat, the want, the desire—the love—just how it used to be between them.

Then he glanced up, said, "I thought we'd better get back to this," and the moment was gone.

Ally managed a nod. *Remember why he's really here.* "Nothing?"

He leaned back in his seat with a frustrated frown. "I don't understand it."

"Keep trying." *Please keep trying.* "I have some work to do." She went to her desk, determined to concentrate on something other than the wild desire to jump him and make sweet love just for the hell of it.

After a productive hour at her computer, she pushed back her chair. "I'm taking a break. You want something to eat?"

At his absent nod, she went into the kitchen. When she returned with drinks and food, Finn was leaning back on the couch, arms behind his head, ankle crossed over one knee, T-shirt straining across his chest. The familiar sight hitched her heart. Yet, despite that nonchalance, she detected unease in his posture, as if the frustration he held such a tight leash on was slipping.

A small photo album was lying across his lap.

"When was this taken?" He pointed to a photo.

She stared. It was a shot of her wearing a wide grin, a short clingy T-shirt and not much else. The lush curve of one hip thrust out against the worn fabric, the outline of her unfettered breasts clearly defined underneath a slogan that declared, "Australian Mushrooms" in tiny print. She looked young, happy and carefree. In love.

The thickness in her throat made it hard to swallow. She put down the tray, unable to meet his eyes. "You'd been working fifteen-hour days and I wanted to give you something personal."

At his raised eyebrow, she clarified. "It was a running joke between us. I once told you that cooking mushrooms smelled like…ah…" She faltered and felt the blush rush up her neck, prickle her skin like tiny needles. "…sex."

"Really."

That one word hung in the air as his eyes darkened imperceptibly, his gaze engulfing her in one possessive sweep.

"So why do *you* have the photo?"

"You returned them after I left." That small betrayal barely hurt anymore, even though she knew he'd been trying to wipe every memory of her from his life. "Cookie?" Without waiting for an answer, she reached for the packet, tore it open and offered one to him.

As Finn slowly crunched on the cookie, Ally put grapes in her mouth, one after the other.

She knew he was watching her beneath hooded eyes, assessing her every move. The unspoken tension slowly increased until she could feel the heat vibrating between them. And when she caught him staring, his gaze was sensual and full of hot knowing. The magic and shock of their impending physical interaction fired between them again, sending her into simultaneous slow smolder and mild panic.

"Well," she said breezily, determinedly cutting off her thoughts, "let's get back to work." *Nothing like a hefty dose of reality to clear all those happy-ever-after fantasies you seem to be having.*

But Finn was obviously on a crusade. "Tell me about your family."

She placed her glass carefully on the coffee table in silence.

"Sit." He patted the seat beside him and she sat, trying to cement her walls of preservation. But they came tumbling back down when he took her shoulders and turned her back to him, then drew long, sensuous fingers through her hair. He gently began to massage her scalp and she moaned softly, inching closer like a small moon caught in the gravitational pull of a mighty planet. She'd never been this close and able to remain aloof. He had that kind of effect on her, primitive and wildly out of control. His strength and determination and passion were everything she'd ever wanted in her life.

How easy this could be, how perfect this little snapshot of domestic bliss was if… *If Finn truly wanted to stay.*

She sighed at the ache in her heart. *Stupid impulsive Ally.*

"My grandfather divorced Grandma Lexie when my mom was a year old," she said softly. "It was quite a scandal—he was from a rich family and she was the housekeeper's daughter. He got custody, then remarried and moved to New Zealand. When Mom turned eighteen she tracked Lexie down, but by then they were poles apart. Mom had hated the good-society-girl role she'd been forced into, and finding her mother was just another way of rebelling against her father's restrictions. Needless to say she got cut from his will. And she's spent all her life trying to 'find herself.'" She made quote marks in the air with her fingers for emphasis, her mouth twitching with sarcasm.

Finn saw her bottom lip stick out, almost as if she was daring him to make a smart comment. Instead he said, "What about your father?"

"Mom met Padraic on an Irish jaunt. They got married and immigrated to Australia before I was born. We lived in the Blue Mountains until I was ten."

"The same time you lost your house."

"Yes." Her eyes rounded at his intuition. "My father was drunk on the lounge, fell asleep while smoking. My mom and I were next door, helping out the neighbors with their new baby." She glanced up at him, then away. "Unlike my father, the house was uninsured. It sounds awful but his death was the best thing that ever happened to Julia."

"Why?"

She groaned softly as his fingers swept over her shoulders to massage her neck, bringing her forward so her warm heat teased and danced into his personal space.

"He was a son of a bitch. For years Mom put up with the constant criticism, the verbal abuse, the stress of living with an alcoholic gambler. My earliest memory is of them arguing. He blamed the bosses who fired him because he screwed up, then the government for a measly pension. He was in denial—yelled at Mom for spending too much and wanting the impossible. As if paying food and utilities was too much to ask."

A small vibration against Finn's thigh had him glancing down. Ally's knee had begun to jiggle a rapid tattoo, her fingers entwining and doing a thread-squeeze-release, thread-squeeze-release over and over. He dragged his gaze from those fingers back to her grim profile.

"Tell me, Ally. It'll help," he finally said, releasing her.

She looked nonplussed. "Who are you? And what have you done with Finn Sørensen?"

"Like I said, I've changed."

"More like regressed. Back into the same man I first met, who says what he feels."

Her admission brought a tight smile to his lips. "I have restrictions in Denmark. Protocols. But here…" He shrugged. "I can't explain it. But I feel more relaxed. More…like myself. Does that sound strange?"

"Not at all. It was something you loved about this country. Anonymity is a wonderful freedom."

They fell silent, and Ally wondered if he was thinking the same thing she was.

"So, you were saying about your family…?"

She sighed, twisting the edge of her pajamas into a tight knot. "Isn't that enough?"

"The greatest influences in our lives come from our parents."

"Now there's a statement."

He leaned back, placing his hands behind his head and

just watched her. Finally she continued. "Padraic laid blame. That's what he did. I can see myself doing it, too, and I hate it."

A small silence, then Finn said, "He's gone, *elskat.*"

"I know. But he's left this…this imprint, as though he hasn't really left at all. I still keep money in the bottom of my wardrobe for a 'rainy day.' I hate to argue, can't stand it when people lie. And as you can see from my mess, I don't get up at the crack of dawn to dust and polish. I need…" *To be needed.* She swallowed that naked confession and instead said, "Julia still runs away from responsibility because my dad made her drag it around for so long."

"What's she like?"

"Still searching for what, I don't know." She shrugged. "I'm pretty sure she never wanted a child, because she left me with Lexie after the insurance came through. I love Julia but—" her chin tilted down, sweeping curtains of curls forward "—I don't understand her. Every birthday I'd wait for a mother who promised to arrive but never did. When she did—months later—it was like a stranger breezing into our lives with gifts and laughter and hope.

"She'd stay a week, maybe two, until she ended up in a row with Lexie, or until the wunderlust got the better of her. And she'd be off the next day. Always promising to be back. Never delivering. I don't know—maybe I'm a reminder of bad things. But it was the story of her life. My dad ignored or lied about his problems, and my mom ran away from hers."

It took her a few seconds to register that Finn was holding her hand, effectively cutting off the nervous wringing she only half realized she'd been doing. She stared at their entwined fingers but didn't pull away.

"You're not like your mother," Finn said gently.

"No?" She raised uncertain eyes to his. "The last time

Mom left I vowed never to let deception ruin my life. I left you because of a lot of things—and one of those was fear. Fear of not being wanted, fear that someone would dig something up and that it would make your family resent me. You're a national celebrity, married to a common, unemployed nobody."

"Ally…" He stroked her fingers, taking simple forbidden pleasure in the intimate contact. "There is nothing common about you. It sounds like Marlene got to you."

"She told the truth."

He leaned over until he could see the rings of dark-blue around her irises. Wondered if he'd ever been so moved by a pair of eyes before, so lost in the complexity of their depth. "Our ancestors were Viking raiders—hardly candidates for modern knighthood. I am a businessman, not a celebrity, and if I wait long enough, another story will take the press's fancy. And you—" he gently tucked a strand of her hair behind her ear "—are the most uncommon woman I have ever met. You're funny, compassionate. Gorgeous."

Her breath hitched as if she had swallowed a laugh. "Gorgeous?"

"Gorgeous," he confirmed. He tipped her chin up, making sure she knew how serious he was. Her involuntary shiver made him smile. "And I'm finding it increasingly hard to resist kissing you again."

Her lips parted, let out a sigh. "So what—" she blinked slowly "—is stopping you?"

He nearly went up in flames right then and there. With his heart thundering away in his chest, he bent forward, meeting her halfway, murmuring against her mouth, "absolutely nothing."

After a few minutes of blissful mouth-on-mouth contact, of soft sighs and gentle rasping of skin on skin, Finn felt her pull away.

"Don't, *elskat.* I want to—"

He never got to finish that sentence because with a small groan, Ally jumped to her feet and ran for the bathroom.

Fourteen

As she threw up into the toilet bowl, Finn gently tapped on the bathroom door.

"In a minute," she gasped, finally sitting back on her heels and wiping her forehead with a damp cloth.

"I've never had this reaction to a kiss before," his muffled reply came through the locked door.

"Funny. You're making jokes while I throw up. Can you just forget this bit ever happened?" She rose slowly to her feet.

"That's my specialty."

She gave a choked laugh and reached for her toothbrush, then unlocked the door.

"Must be coming down with something," she muttered and stuck the brush in her mouth.

"I told you you were warm." His concerned gaze swept over her and Ally was suddenly aware that she was standing there in a pair of ratty drawstring pajama bottoms and a spaghetti-strap tank with a too-tight front.

When he met her eyes, her heart fluttered, tightening just a little more. His gentle expression quickened her breath until she forced herself to take a slower one. Everything depended on keeping a tight rein on her feelings. If she slipped up, certain heartbreak lurked just around the corner.

She didn't want to think about that.

He reached out, gently tugged the useless band from her hair and retied it back. A small shot of panic hit her low and hard. She vigorously upped the pace on her brushing.

After a while he said, "You should go to bed."

"I'm okay," she lied, rinsing her mouth and spitting into the sink.

"You look tired. Go. This can wait until morning. I'll go get my stuff from the hotel."

Without an argument, she nodded. "Okay. The couch pulls out into a bed. I'll get you some sheets."

When Finn returned, she'd pulled out the couch and fixed up the sheets. "It may not be five-star, but it's comfortable. Well—" Ally shoved her hair behind her ears. "—sleep well."

As she turned to leave, his soft question stopped her in her tracks.

"No goodnight kiss?"

She threw a look over her shoulder. "You're deluded."

"Just a little one?" He grinned.

"You're awfully sure of yourself."

The look of heated mischief in his eyes was one she hadn't seen in a long time, but still, oh, so familiar. "What I'm sure of is our attraction, *elskat*. If you weren't trying so hard to fight it, you'd see it, too."

* * *

The next morning they reviewed every minute detail again, from Ally's time line to the last of the letters and notes, until Ally was numb with the constant battering of her sagging defenses.

Her control and objectivity began to slip. An annoying little voice inside had taken up residence, demanding to know what had happened to the kissing bit. She tried to ignore it but it only got louder. It was absolutely no help that Finn sat within touchable distance, looking better than any guy had a right to.

Her restraint was treading a precarious tightrope over a river of lust and she wasn't entirely sure she could stay focused.

With their wedding photos spread before them and a black lump of sadness in her heart, she leaned forward to ease the kink in her back.

"Maybe we're concentrating too hard." She rolled her neck and sighed.

Finn's eagle gaze picked up that movement. "How are you feeling?"

"Nothing that a massage couldn't fix," she joked. But when he stood and reached down for her hand, she shook her head in alarm.

"Yes," he argued and nudged her. "Sit on the footstool and I'll give you a massage."

Reluctantly she sat and leaned forward so her elbows rested on her knees. With a feeling half of trepidation, half of anticipation, Finn sat on the chair behind her and slowly peeled up her tank to reveal the smooth skin of her lower back.

He gritted his teeth. *Focus on something else. Projected business plans. Profit and loss reports. The annual general meeting.* And he pretended not to notice the way she nearly jumped a foot in the air when he touched her.

Two minutes later he was mentally reciting the World Cup winners from present to past when she groaned. If that wasn't enough to gnaw at his thin control, she had to go and sigh, then rotate her neck and drop her head back.

The tempting smell of her hair, the satin curls as they swished at him—back and forth as she rolled her neck—grabbed hold of his libido and squeezed.

His body's response was electric, as though all the elements had gathered together and were now warring beneath his skin. His groin hardened with sudden painful intensity and his breath snagged, throat dry with desire and heat.

She suddenly twisted, eyes wide, and a small squeak—suspiciously like another groan—escaped.

He stared at her profile, then her lips. And stayed there.

He couldn't remember when he'd last felt this content to just *be* with someone.

His hands paused then slowly began to creep around to her stomach.

She jumped as if he'd burnt her, frantically pulling down her shirt as she put distance between them.

The lust in his brain crashed to the floor. She didn't want him. Her response was evidence enough.

Again, he'd forced her into a situation. He groaned and pinched the bridge of his nose, the emotional push-pull sending a sharp pain to the back of his eyes.

"Finn…" she whispered.

"Mmmm."

"I do feel it."

He didn't pretend to misunderstand. He looked up at her, standing alone and vulnerable beside the couch. It wrenched his heart. Mutely he nodded.

The tension in her shoulders seemed to ease off a bare inch. "It's just… I'm…"

"What?"

"I'm so—"

"Hot?"

"Conflicted."

"I know."

"And aroused."

Now with his full attention, she gave him a weary smile. "But as much as I'm attracted, I can't let myself get hurt again. You understand?"

He nodded. "Maybe we're trying too hard. On my memory, that is."

Was it his imagination or did she look relieved? "That... sounds logical."

"So we should... I'll..." Dammit, why was it so hard to say? He scowled, stuck his hands in his pockets.

As if sensing his awkwardness, she came to his rescue. "Take the car for a few hours. I need to do some work here anyway."

He gave a curt nod and without another word, turned for the door.

Fifteen

Two weeks later, on Saturday night, Ally eyed her reflection in the mirror with annoyance. The Boobs From Hell, that's what she was. What had once been a perfectly good after-five dress had turned into a prop from a Fellini film. No matter which way she turned, they were there. Straining at the seams. Looking…well…huge.

The soft knock on her bedroom door stopped Ally mid-adjustment. "Come in."

Finn walked in with a shopping bag, then abruptly stopped. He cleared his throat.

"Are you actually going to wear that?"

She put her hands on her hips and scowled, daring him to comment.

"You have a problem with my dress?"

Finn let his gaze roam leisurely over her curves poured into a cherry-red sheath that, given another time and place, he would have been more than happy to see her in. Or out of. Creamy breasts straining against satin material, barely keeping themselves decent. A come-hither figure more compelling than a takeover bid.

He tore his fascinated gaze from the glorious sight, slowly dragging his eyes up to her face. Her chin shot up, along with her eyebrows, and she looked so indignant he couldn't resist.

"*Elskat,* every man in the room will have a problem once they see you."

She struggled to remain offended but he detected a glimmer of a smile tugging her lips.

The moment spun out, seemed to lengthen.

In the last couple of weeks he'd discovered depths to Ally that he hadn't foreseen. Her undeniable passion and the intimacy they shared was a constant wonder to him, as if their darkest times together had somehow brought a new understanding, a new facet to their relationship. She no longer flinched when he took her hand. No longer balked at his gentle touch on her arm or her back as he guided her through a crowd.

Yet he also knew she was confused with the changes she saw in him. The Finn of the past would never have done half the things they'd done.

Especially not suggesting that they use sex to get his memory back.

Yet *she* was frustrating *him* because he saw right through her I-know-what-I-want declaration. Like claiming aloofness but letting her eyes linger when she thought he wasn't looking. Saying she was happy with her life when it was so clearly a mess. Telling him she wasn't physically interested, then agreeing to his wild theory—a theory that had only gone as far as a few mind-blowing kisses.

She'd let him into her home and he'd moved his meager belongings into the space as if he'd been there for months.

And gradually, with every hour he spent with her, the person he was supposed to be—the rich businessman who was hell-bent on finding the truth no matter what—was sliding further and further from his memory.

His headaches were less frequent, the unyielding tension in his muscles easing off for hours at a time. And the bliss of sleep…

It was like some relaxant seeping into his bones, calming him.

He didn't have the energy to miss the old Finn. That man had felt all wrong, as if he'd known all along who he was inside, yet was forced to conform to expectations on the outside. Ally had played a major part in that realization with her passion and attitude and come-to-bed body. She'd pushed all his buttons, made him question his purpose.

He'd love nothing better than to be right here. With Ally. Living together as man and wife.

Astonished, he let that revelation wash over him. Wishful thinking or distinct possibility? And what would Ally say? Do? Plus, there was the small matter of that codicil….

At her questioning gaze, he held out the bag he was carrying. "I bought you something. A good-luck present."

Eyeing the bag with suspicion, she finally pulled out the box. And when she lifted the lid, reverently lifted out the blue dress she'd tried on two weeks ago, and raised her eyes to his, he released the breath he'd been holding.

"Finn," she said softly, his name wondrous delight on her lips. "You shouldn't—"

"I wanted to." He took a step closer as she held it up and studied herself in the full-length mirror. "I also want to give you this."

He produced a long velvet box. She stared at it, dumbfounded.

"Open it," he urged.

Slowly she eased back the lid, then gasped. On a bed of

navy velvet lay a delicate silver and blue sapphire necklace.
The blue stones were square cut, tinier than her pinky finger-
nail, alternating between links of polished silver. In the
middle, a single round blue teardrop sapphire dangled,
winking in the light.

"Louisa designed it for next season's collection. I had it
couriered."

He took it from her, gently placed it around her neck and
fastened the clip.

Speechless, she stared at the necklace in the mirror, finger-
ing the stones, the graceful sweep of the links as they lay
against her skin. Then she looked up at him and his hand went
to her cheek, stroking the soft curve.

He heard the breath catch in her throat. "I don't deserve…"

"You deserve to be dressed in silks, to be treated like
royalty. You deserve to feel good about yourself, especially
tonight." His hand dropped to her shoulder, stroking the warm
flesh under his fingers. "Let me make you feel good, *kæreste*.
I promise you won't be disappointed."

True to his word he'd made Ally feel good all the way to
Fox Studios. He'd actually hired a stretch limousine and spent
the journey leisurely licking fizzy lemonade from her lips
every time she took a sip from the champagne flute.

Her mouth still tingled from his particular brand of "feel
good." Her skin, however, itched as if she'd scrubbed it within
an inch of its life, her breasts ached and her stomach was queasy.

When the chauffeur opened her door, Ally froze. The
sudden whir and flash of cameras smacked her in the face, the
roar of the crowd rising to a deafening pitch. A roped-off red
carpet lay dead ahead, flanked by reporters. Behind them a
sea of onlookers strained at the barriers, desperate to catch a
glimpse of the limo's occupants.

As quickly as the déjà vu moment came, it disappeared when Finn leaned down and took her hand. "Smile, *elskat.* It's your night."

He helped her out and guided her down the carpet, smiling and waving as if it were a natural part of breathing.

It is, she thought. She, meanwhile, couldn't get over the fact that she was in the company of celebrities, would be rubbing shoulders with TV stars, movie directors, newspaper moguls and models.

Security ushered them through the heavy double doors of the Hall of Industries, into a huge room decorated like the heavens above. Walls of sky blue depicted dozens of floating clouds, tiny star lights wound around tall marble columns and the waiters were all dressed in togas and sandals, complete with halos and wings.

"Wow." Ally absorbed the scenery with an awe-filled gasp as Finn squeezed her hand. A gasp that was cut short when she spotted Simon, who, in turn, spotted them.

"Ally! PR told me you were coming. Wouldn't miss it for the world." He turned to Finn who was standing silently by her side. "We weren't properly introduced last time. Simon Carter. Ally's boss."

"Ex-boss," Ally amended tightly as they shook hands.

"Finn Sørensen," Finn said.

Ally could see Simon's brain working overtime. "You related to that Danish jewelry designer?"

"He was my father."

Simon nodded, turned to Ally to kiss her cheek in greeting, but she moved backward into the warm strength of Finn. She was shaking inside, hating Simon for lying to her and cornering them so publicly, hating the fact that Finn was a witness to the results of her own naïveté.

"Sørensen Silver makes classy stuff." He eyeballed her

necklace appreciatively. "Which reminds me—" there was an unflattering gleam in his eye "—how come you don't wear a ring?"

"It's being custom-made," she answered quickly before Finn could turn his dark frown into something more verbal. Everything inside revolted at this confrontation, refused to accept Simon's false politeness in any shape or form. Disgust was a bitter taste on the tip of her tongue.

As Finn turned and smiled to someone who called a passing greeting, Simon bent low so only she could hear.

"Great to see you here, Ally."

"And *you* lied."

He smiled humourlessly and shrugged. "Desperate measures."

"And lucky you—I've saved you from the wrath of Max. Certainly wasn't my intention, but…"

He took a step forward, way inside her comfort zone. "For the sake of your career, I'd advise you to play nice, Ally."

"It seems you have a problem with bullying women, Carter. Or is it just my wife?"

Finn looked dangerous, like an avenging angel swooping in to her rescue as he pulled her back, shielding her with his muscular shoulder. His eyes promised bodily harm and his fists clenched by his sides. As the strobe light spliced across his face, his body tensed, ready for action.

His sheer physical presence took Ally's breath away.

Simon stepped back and opened his mouth to say something more.

Finn made a sound low in his throat, moving closer so that his meaning could not be misinterpreted. "Is this worth more than your pretty face, Carter? I will flatten you if you persist in hounding my wife. Try explaining a bloody nose to the cameras."

Simon's eyes widened and he hastily took another step

backward. He seemed to pull himself together, swallowed whatever he was about to say and retreated behind that polished veneer Ally knew so well.

"We're done here," Simon muttered and turned on his heel.

Ally tugged on Finn's arm and when he looked down, his eyes still full of fury, she astounded him with a soft kiss. "Thank you."

No one had come to her defense before, she thought with a little inner glow. She'd always been the one to take care of herself. The strong one, the take-charge girl.

As if he understood that, he swept the back of his hand over her cheek, so gently that her breath caught painfully in her chest. She laced her fingers through his.

"He knows who you are," she stated unnecessarily.

"That does not matter."

"But—"

"It feels good that you worry for me, *elskat*—" he smiled down at her "—but I cannot hide forever. Better it be on my terms than someone else's."

She felt the tension seep from her body as he brought his lips to hers in a tender kiss. "I'm here, that's all that matters. Now enjoy your night."

Ally prayed her nausea would stay away and she'd make it through the ceremony without throwing up on anyone important. To her amazement her prayers were answered. She even managed a joke or two with the young, hunky presenter and made a thank-you speech she distinctly remembered only as, "*mmmrrrggrrrrpp*. Thanks!"

Now, with the celebrations well underway, the warmth of the packed room began to press urgently around, the thumping beat of the dance-floor music pounding heavily in her throat.

Shifting from foot to foot, she leaned up against a cloud-covered wall as she waited in line to use the bathroom. She was so tired, even her bones ached. All that smiling and socializing had really taken it out of her, not to mention avoiding Simon all night. She absently ran a palm over her stomach just as the snap and flash of cameras went off in her face.

She turned to give the photographer a mouthful but Finn appeared beside her. "Smile, *skat*. The cameras are watching. Again."

"This was a dumb idea," she said through a wide smile and clenched teeth as another guy took her picture.

"No, it wasn't. You got this—" he waved the elégant crystal award he held "—and had a great time. They all loved you."

"I suppose they did," she said grudgingly. "Dammit, what takes women so long in the bathroom?" She quickly glanced around. "Wait here, I'll be just a sec." She marched over to the men's room.

After she'd used the facilities, she swung open the stall door to find a man washing his hands at the sink.

"Oh! I'm sorry, but the line outside was—"

The man grabbed a towel and turned. "Miss McKnight." To her mortification, she realized it was Max Bowman, *Bliss's* editor-in-chief. "I've been meaning to talk to you all night."

She stepped back, blushing furiously. "About?"

He smiled, threw the towel into the basket and readjusted his sleeves. "Your job. Let's go outside."

Ally's head spun with incredulity as she finally made her way back to Finn. Max had just offered her her old position back with a hefty increase in salary. And heaven help her, she was seriously thinking about taking it. *I need a job. I can't live on my savings forever.*

Finn's keen eyes took in her pinched expression. "Problem?"

She shrugged. "Just tired. Can we get out of here?"

"Sure."

Finn took her elbow and skillfully guided them through the throng with breathtaking speed, then out the door.

Cool air hit her warm face, goose-bumping her skin.

"Wait here." He stroked her arm. "I will organize our car." As he strode over to the parking attendant hovering in the background, she sensed someone behind her.

"Just wanted to congratulate you," Simon's voice cut in.

"Thanks." Ally glanced at Finn who was returning, now with a scowl as he spotted Simon. "Well, we must be going."

"Sure."

With a sigh of relief, Ally looped her arm through Finn's and they began to move down the steps.

"Oh, geez, I'm an idiot!" Simon slapped his forehead. "Congratulations, mate."

With a tempered sigh, Finn paused and turned. "For…?"

It was in that precise moment that Ally realized everything was about to crumble. She glanced backward and watched Simon's slow, oily smile spread, an expression of nasty delight on his face.

For one gut-lurching second, she was above them all, looking down on the scene in horror. The sheer panic in her face magnified the significance of the moment.

"Man. Have I gone and put my foot in it?" Simon's mouth stretched wider. "Sorry about that, Ally. Guess you were keeping the bundle of joy a surprise." When he looked pointedly at her stomach she drew a protective hand across it, playing right into his game. "Still, no one would've guessed in that dress." He looked up, right into Finn's frozen face. "Well, enjoy fatherhood. Better you than me."

Ally squeezed her eyes shut, eliminating Simon's retreating back and wishing she could disappear just as quickly. She knew the instant Finn had figured it out—his arm stiffened from the blow. Then, more alarmingly, she felt his whole body grow rigid, as if ice had frozen in his veins.

"Ally?"

"What?" She trembled at the arctic voice, opening her eyes to a horrible unyielding expression on his face.

"You're pregnant." Those green eyes were full of complex emotion. Betrayal, disappointment. And white-hot accusation.

Damn him. "Don't you dare judge me, Finn. Don't you dare."

"You're pregnant." His eyes grazed her waist then returned to her face. If a look could have burned, she'd be toast.

She tilted her chin up. "Yes."

"To Simon."

She recoiled. "No! It's…" *Oh, dammit.* A sob hitched in her throat as her voice cracked. With a heavy sense of impending doom, she prayed for strength, swallowing her last shred of resistance. "It's yours."

Nothing could have prepared her for the utter disbelief on his face. Nothing could have cut her to the bone more.

Seconds seemed to pass by in a matter of hours, the complete and total silence echoing the shallow breath coming from his frozen countenance.

"I'm…going to be a father?" he said slowly, his voice shaking with discovery.

She nodded mutely.

He muffled a groan, dragging a hand over his eyes. Ally could only stand and wring her hands. What was he going to say? Do? The uncertainty spun her thoughts in a thousand different directions, all of them desperate and implausible.

The car pulled up then and in the next second he composed himself, his noble, proud features settling into controlled restraint.

She yanked open the door and crawled in, desperate to be

alone with him, to explain. Yet Finn remained outside, rooted to the spot.

"Are you getting in?" Ally asked tentatively.

"No."

"But—"

With a withering look he slammed the door, the force of the impact rattling the windows.

Sixteen

As though a thousand demons from his Viking past were hot on his heels, Finn stormed along the promenade that ran parallel to Coogee Beach. Stretching out, he took long, frustrated strides as the walking track sloped steeply upwards toward the cliffs, uncaring of the overgrown grass occasionally stabbing his legs or of the hectic pace he'd set.

The sea air whipped around him, the morning sun angrily beat down until sweat broke out on his brow. He squinted as his eyes watered.

And still he could see Ally's face, hear those two words confirming that unbelievable revelation.

A baby. Ally's baby.

His baby.

In his mind, he pictured her, her belly growing big and round with child. Her body blossoming, swelling with the evidence of their passion and love.

The rage in him grew, feeding and festering until his head spun. Shards of pain stabbed behind his eyes, blinding.

His baby.

Instead of fading out, the words reverberated in his head, growing louder with every cheerful seagull call. With every low whoosh of the surf against the rocks below.

The air was suddenly sucked from his lungs as though someone had turned on a giant vacuum. With a choke, Finn squeezed his eyes shut as pain sliced the back of his head.

His body throbbed from lack of air and he took a deep breath, then another, trying to force control through the pain. Fuzzy snapshots of memory raced past—Ally furious and accusing, in tears. Him yelling straight back, uncaring.

…baby….

It was like clawing his way out of a dream, only to find that he'd been awake the whole time. Bits and pieces came flashing back indiscriminately: their hasty marriage at that corny Las Vegas chapel, her love of chocolate fudge cake. Her disastrous but hilarious attempt to cook him a traditional Danish meal.

I need to think.

The images abruptly snapped.

He gasped for breath, feeling the trickle of sweat at the back of his neck, the throbbing ache flooding into every muscle. Shaking his head, he tried to rid himself of the sharp insistent ringing in his ears.

With a deep shuddering breath he ground the heels of his hands into his eyes.

"You okay, mate?" a passing male voice drifted in.

He didn't look up. "Yeah. Thanks."

You're losing it. He massaged the back of his neck, trying to force back a steadily pounding headache. Through sheer force of will he shoved unwelcome images from his head and instead focused on his breathing, taking steady, slow lungfuls of air.

After another five minutes he felt calm enough to think.

He remembered. Not everything, not the codicil. But enough to make sense of who he had been and how he was so different now.

He was going to be a father.

Fear inched its way across his shoulders, slid down his spine. What kind of father would he be? Like his dad, an obsessed workaholic who barely had time for his wife, let alone his son? Like his former self?

Since when have you complained about your lot in life? Nikolai's booming voice of logic echoed in his brain. *You love your work and the lifestyle it gives you.*

No. It wasn't like that. *He* wasn't like that.

Yet he couldn't banish the pictures from his head—those memories, his father's last words, his friends' and colleagues' accounts of his past life.

Ally's cold reaction to his arrival.

Everything came back to her, despite his determined attempts to rationalize and explain away his attraction. Even without steady income, even pregnant, Ally was so determined not to need anyone. Least of all him.

But there was no way he could pretend this didn't change everything.

He continued along the path, tearing off a broken stalk of pampas grass as he strode past, swishing it against his thigh like a riding crop.

She needed this money now, more than anything. Which meant now, more than ever, he had to find that codicil.

A bend in the track forced him to grind to a halt. As though a lightning bolt had cleaved the earth centuries ago, the land dropped off abruptly into the blue expanse of the Pacific Ocean. The waves pounded onto the rocky outcrops below, spouting foam and sea spray. The sun rained down, the fires of his own private hell.

He didn't know how long he stood there, staring out to sea with the tiny itchy prickles straining, those familiar ants crawling over his skin. He only knew that when he finally acknowledged the breeze cooling his sweaty skin, the sun was well and truly high in the sky.

And with the sting of blood in his veins pounding with loss and regret that no amount of concentration could lessen, anger slowly gave way to purpose.

With his jaw set tighter than an overpumped football, he spun and headed back.

Seventeen

Standing a block from her building after picking up the morning paper, Ally spotted Finn. She watched him cut a tall, determined figure through the late-morning throng on Coogee Bay Road, striding as if he'd got her in the crosshairs and had honed right on in, completely focused on his quarry. She roped in her own nervousness, gathering it around like a protective cloak.

You need to keep a level head if you want any chance of staying in control.

Finally he stopped in front of her, the sharp planes of his face emphasizing the steely glint in his eyes.

"The baby is mine."

It wasn't a question. Ally nodded curtly. "Yes."

"Did I know about it?"

"No."

"Why not?"

Ally glanced around. "Not here." She turned and headed back to the apartment, not waiting to see if he followed.

When they were finally alone, Ally watched Finn with a wary eye.

She'd never seen him grapple so hard for control, despite all their passionate arguments. He couldn't keep still, pacing up and down, back and forth, back and forth, until he finally ended up at the patio. Drawing the doors open, he took a long, deep breath, drinking in the fresh air as if he'd been suffocating.

"Why didn't you tell me?" he finally asked, his back still to her.

"What purpose would it have served?"

He spun, sudden fury tightening his jaw. "What about my right to know? Were you ever going to tell me? Or are you really that selfish?"

Pain of the past, fragmented memories, tore and twisted, drawing blood.

"Selfish? I didn't know I was pregnant until I came home. I did think about telling you, a million times a day. But you never wanted children. What would you have done in my place?"

"Don't you put this on me, Ally."

"Well it *is* on you! You'd always said the company was a major part of your life, but I didn't realize how major until it was too late." *I tried to hate the company but settled for a flesh-and-blood man instead.* "You said quite clearly 'I don't want children.' I knew you'd never budge. End of story."

There was tension in the sudden stillness. Ally watched him clench and unclench his fists until his knuckles turned white.

The expression on his face was ominous, the rumbling gathering of imminent storm clouds. Tightly coiled emotion swept his body as if someone had just primed him and now he was ready to fire.

Ally crossed her arms and waited.

"That baby needs a father," he stated.

Of all the things to say, it was the least she expected. "In case you haven't noticed, this *is* the twenty-first century. There's nothing wrong with being a single parent."

"You misunderstand me, Ally." His eyes narrowed. "I will not sit by and let your life fall to pieces."

Outrage blurred her vision. "Oh, and you think you know how to fix it, do you? It's my life and I'm not giving this baby up. What kind of person do you think I am?"

"For a smart woman, you can be extremely thick sometimes. There will be no divorce."

Total shock rendered her argument to a wordless splutter.

"What?" Finn smiled thinly, "Finally lost for words?"

She breathed deeply, trying to cut off the simultaneous hope and dread. "Well, here's one. No."

"You forget you have nothing," he murmured.

"And you forget what we did to each other! If, by some smidgen of insanity I agreed, what makes you think this time would be any different? I'm not leaving and you don't belong here," she reminded him bluntly. "Your home is in Denmark and I will not be your reason for staying."

"You can't get rid of me. If you try, I will fight you. And I'll win."

With that one vow, Ally was engulfed in a wave that left her floundering in the aftermath. It was more than a physical pain, it was a deep, glancing blow to her soul. All the memories, all of Finn's past traits that she'd thought were finally gone, were reflected clearly on his face, in every muscle of his rigid stance. The cold depths in his eyes, the stubborn challenge of his tight jaw. It was a don't-mess-with-me look that she knew all too well. Her stomach bottomed out.

"We entered into this agreement knowing it was temporary," she finally said.

"I did not know all the facts," he pointedly reminded her. "If you think I will walk out on my responsibilities—"

"It's a child, Finn, not just a responsibility. And, yes, I fully expect you to honor your agreement and leave when this is over. I don't want anything more from you than what we agreed on."

The leashed tension on his face gave way to something…sad. Something painful and betrayed. As if she'd delivered a swift slap of reality. The look of self-directed anger was tightly controlled as he swept his jaw with his palm.

Then she blinked and he was back to being the resolute, stubborn Finn of old.

It fired her determination even more.

"I'm not broken, Finn, so stop trying to fix me." With adrenaline flushing her cheeks she marched right up to him, put her hands on her hips and thrust her chin out. "Contrary to what you think, I'm perfectly capable of making my own decisions."

"It is my child, too. Don't forget that."

"Believe me, there's been times I've wished I could!"

Fury blazed from his eyes. "What's that supposed to mean?"

"Do you think I enjoyed throwing away a marriage? That I wanted us to break up? That I didn't try every second of every damn day to make it work? But I couldn't, Finn. I couldn't try anymore. We broke up, I came home, then discovered I was pregnant. But you had a new girlfriend. A new life. There was no way I would shove either of us back into that mess. And this child is better off with one loving parent than two miserable ones."

Like two wary animals they faced each other off, one bristling and indignant, one guarded and stubborn, until something passed between them: a look, a feeling from the past that wasn't quite dead. Something primal and deep.

"I'm finished with this," she announced, impatiently shoving her hair back. "You're here to get your memory back, not make new ones."

He grabbed her chin and forced her eyes to his. "Stop running away."

"And stop assuming I need your help." She yanked away from his grip.

"I'm not the same person I was. I've changed."

Enough to stay? She refused to voice that cursed question aloud. It brought back too many heartbreaks, too many buried arguments and Lord knew, she didn't want to argue anymore.

The silence suddenly became heavy with unsaid words and denied attraction, like a dark storm cloud swollen with rain.

"I think," he murmured, "you're just as determined to push me away as I am to help you. You have no steady income. No place to raise a child—a small apartment doesn't compare to a proper house. And yet you still resist my offer. Why?"

Because when you finally remember, I'll lose you all over again.

His eyes softened as if reading her thoughts. "*Elskat.* I promise I won't hurt you."

"You've said *that* before."

He took a step forward, almost as if he wanted to reach out and hold her, but stopped abruptly, unsure of her response.

"I can't compete with your company, Finn. Can't you see we'd only end up hating each other?" *Again,* she added silently. Dropping her hand to her stomach, she took a deep breath. "I ran once. How do you know I won't run again?"

She thought she saw a flash of emotion cross those world-weary planes of his face—part pain, part regret. The Finn she'd known was strictly no regrets. But what about this man standing across from her? She could read the doubt in his face, feel it in the way the silence lengthened between them.

"I don't want you to promise something you can't give," she finally said, turning toward the kitchen.

"I can give you money—"

"*Especially* money."

He followed her, pausing in the doorway. "Dammit, Ally, it is my child. Why won't you let me help you?"

"Because I don't want it!" She slammed two coffee cups onto the countertop with a crack and whirled to face him.

"Because your pride won't allow it." She took a step back into the countertop as he came at her slowly, deliberately. "Where's your pride when you're hungry, with a mountain of bills to pay? Babies aren't cheap, you know. There's medical expenses, insurance, day-to-day living. Cots and diapers and clean sheets—"

"Stop it!"

He grabbed her shoulders, almost as if he meant to shake some sense into her.

"I don't want your help!" She shook herself free with a jerk. "I've been looking after myself since I was ten. I don't need someone else to take control."

"This isn't about me needing control. Do not test my patience." The look in those emerald-green depths was dangerous, full of warning and hot anger. "You avoid my questions, lie to me—"

"Don't analyze me, Finn. I don't lie."

"But you *do* leave out details. The baby. Your parents. And then there's the real reason why you left our marriage."

Fear clogged her throat, making her breath come out raspy until she managed to gain control. "I told you. We've been over this."

"And I'm not buying it."

She crossed her arms protectively. "I was lonely, depressed. Homesick. I felt—" she grappled for the right words, desperate to make him understand, "—alone in a crowded room."

"So after three months of marriage you just up and quit."

"That's it." She reached for the cutlery drawer, pulled out two spoons. "I gave up, straight after your no-child declaration. Is that what you want to hear?"

"The woman in those letters was in love, completely committed and determined to make our marriage work. She wouldn't have just given up on that."

She turned on him, grateful for the anger that fuelled her indignation. "I left everything behind to be with you, not to visit museums and historical attractions by myself. Not to play second fiddle to your father's company. And not to fall asleep at night without you, then wake up in an empty bed. How much longer was I supposed to torture myself? I spent my childhood being ignored by my parents and I wasn't going to let that happen again. Sure, I believed love could conquer everything—in the beginning. Boy, was I wrong."

He refused to jump to the bait, instead remaining diplomatically silent.

Yet the war he was waging inside reflected clearly in his eyes, on his face and suddenly, despite all those words they'd thrown at each other, she felt regret creep in.

She swallowed and softened her voice. "You were right." She turned away to put the spoons in the cups, then pulled out a couple of plates. "You said your work was a major part of your life and the culture shock would be enormous. But I also discovered my own individual identity suddenly didn't matter. I hated how I was expected to act a certain way, do certain things because of who you were. And I hated how you'd lied to me." She opened the refrigerator and took out the milk. "I handled it badly. It was…the type of person I was then."

She grabbed the coffeepot with more annoyance than care and poured. Hot coffee slopped over the cup, scalding her hand.

With a soft curse she slammed the pot down then brought the throbbing skin to her mouth and sucked. "I didn't try hard enough. I know that. I was desperate to fit in, to belong. But I was a poor foreigner, not suitable for you. So with every 'you must make an effort' I was subtly frozen out."

She'd hated Finn for his demands, his high expectations. His refusal to understand how difficult it was to fit in, to work at being accepted. She'd hated the shy, insecure person she'd become because of her all-consuming love for one man.

"Ally," he said now, his voice so soft she barely heard it with all the thoughts tumbling about in her head.

"What?"

He took her burned hand and swept his palm over the red skin. She tried to pull back but he held on fast. And when she dared to look up, he was so close she could see the small flecks of gold ringing his pupils, see those long lashes that used to close in passion when she kissed him—

"I'm sorry," he said.

"It was just… I didn't…" She ended with a sigh, letting him rinse her hand under the cold-water faucet. "Look, I was young and insecure and felt betrayed. And you…"

"I was proud and refused to chase after you." He dabbed at her skin with a clean towel.

She nodded slowly. "Yes."

He released her, stuck his hands in his pockets and hunched those broad shoulders. "Thanks for being honest."

Not completely, her conscience niggled. "If you're not honest with yourself, you could end up living a life you don't want."

"Do you have a life you want now?"

Yes. No. I don't know any more. She settled for a shrug and felt his eyes graze her, almost like a physical caress.

"Ally." Finn wanted to touch her again but she turned back to the sink, effectively dismissing him. In very subtle ways, she'd been dismissing him—no, *rejecting* him since he'd gotten here. Her walls of self-protection were so solid that he was unsure of how to breech them.

Then she sniffed.

Dammit, was she crying? "Does your hand hurt?"

"No."

With all the thrust of a newly sharpened knife, her watery denial cut into his stomach and twisted. He had made her cry.

"Please turn around," he said softly.

"Why?"

"Because I need to see your face."

"No, you don't. You forgot about me, remember?" Her laugh came out strangled. "Of course you don't remember. Stupid question."

His hands on her shoulders were so gentle that at first, Ally didn't feel it. When he grasped her more firmly, turned her to face him, she glared at him and set her jaw.

"Don't. I…" But Ally couldn't say another word because the look in his emerald-green eyes undid her. His gaze reflected emotion so deep, so powerful that it nearly winded her. Something she couldn't quite place…

He was right. He was so different to the man she had once known it was as if a stranger stood before her. Where he'd been quick to lay blame and freeze her out, now she only saw a man needing answers. A man wanting to support his child and getting frustrated by her less-than-honest responses.

And to her complete mortification, she felt the soft track of tears slide down her cheeks.

She tried to force herself to stop, but that only made it worse. Finn had hated to see her cry. It made him angry and defensive. Once he'd accused her of emotional manipulation. So she'd done it in private, alone. He'd never known.

"It's the hormones." She attempted a smile and ducked her face, but he reached up and brushed her damp skin with a gentle stroke of his thumb pad. The shock and pleasure jump-started every single vein in her body.

She didn't want to stare at his mouth but she couldn't look away. She didn't want to imagine kissing him, but her thoughts were seized with the memories of a thousand aching kisses. And when she brought her gaze up to his again, it was as if he had read her very thoughts because suddenly, his lips came crashing down onto hers.

His skin smelled like every memory she still had of him, all of them hot. Sexual. His lips tasted of heat and forbidden promises. His hands engulfed her face and, mouth on mouth, their breaths mingled, then their tongues.

Her senses erupted with familiar awareness and longing as he pulled her closer to his warm, hard body, caressed and stroked her back, wrapped his arms around her.

Ally gave one desperate moan and knew she was lost. It was like coming home after being away for an eternity.

Every nerve ending crackled, every inch of her skin was alert and craving to be touched. A thin sheen of sweat broke out and trickled down the small of her back as reality and memory entwined—those deep soul kisses, the soft intimate touches. And those lazy mornings making love...

Somewhere in the back of her mind the warning signs began to clamor feebly. Danger, danger. Don't let him stroke your neck. Don't let him—oh, my!—suck on your bottom lip or nibble your jaw or let those warm hands creep under your shirt and touch your...

Ally jumped, drawing in a sharp breath as his expert fingers stroked the sensitive skin of her gently rounded abdomen. She didn't want to get used to this again—his kisses, his touch. Get used to having him in her life when she knew he would eventually turn right back around and leave again.

Even as common sense sent out all the warning signs, she couldn't think straight with his mouth pressed to her neck while his hot, skilled hands unsnapped the buttons on her pants.

She was past the point of caring anymore.

When his palm curled around her hip, she stiffened. "Finn… I…"

"Don't, *elskat.* There's nothing you need to hide from me."

Oh, God. That old, worn endearment felt like rain to her parched throat. She groaned in frustration as the last remnants of her iron will came crumbling down.

And still Finn was doing things that made her body sing with pleasure. Warm arousal spiraled between her legs as he continued his kissing, stroking, teasing. She let him. She let him put his mouth wherever he wanted, over every inch of her craving skin. Let him peel up her shirt and trail those magic hands toward one sensitive breast.

Her knees buckled. She could do nothing but cling to him, a drowning being on a sea of desire. How many nights had she dreamt of this? How many days had she spent desperately wanting to be back in his arms, in his life? In his bed?

Another moan dragged from her lips, ending on a sigh when he dipped his head and gently bit her nipple through the thin satin of her bra.

"Finn. We have to…"

He raised heavy-lidded eyes to hers. The passion in them blew her away. "*Kæreste,* please don't tell me to stop. I don't think I can."

"My shirt," she got out. "Take it off. Quick."

The look on his face was worth a thousand heartaches. He yanked her shirt over her head and she heard a seam give way.

Then they were clawing at each other like two eager teenagers, exchanging hungry kisses. Groping. Tasting. Teasing.

Half undressed, Finn pulled Ally into the living room and down onto the rug.

"For months I've been having these dreams," he murmured, hot in her ear. "I saw you naked, lying on a rug exactly like this one. Making love to you." The soft acrylic fur enveloped them both, a thousand sensual fingers tickling every inch of exposed flesh. "Moving inside you. You were all warm and wet."

Ally let her eyes close, reveling in the feel of his hands on her body, the rug's feathery decadence on her back and bottom, his hot, urgent kisses on her breasts.

Her fingers dived into his hair and held on as she whispered sweet words of encouragement. And when she took a deep breath he was in her senses completely—the bittersweet memory of his cologne, musky skin and faint sheen of sweat that was so typically Finn.

Almost wondrously, she swept her palms over his shoulders and down his arms, discovering the swell of bicep and sinew and hard male. She had missed this so much, this touching. She placed soft feathery kisses on his nape and he shuddered. She'd also missed having this seductive power over a man—this man. Missed feeling the sweet tremble her kisses, her touch, could evoke. It was humbling and empowering all at once.

His hand slid down to the juncture of her thighs, eyes registering a silent question. He needn't have asked. She willingly parted for him. As his fingers unerringly found the hot center of her arousal, she gasped, her hips instinctively jerking up, writhing for his touch.

Gently he rubbed his thumb across her most sensitive part, again and again until Ally's breath became ragged. Trembling, she clamped her teeth down on her lip to stop from crying aloud.

"Don't hold back, *elskat,*" he said, kissing her. "Open your eyes."

She couldn't refuse him—could never refuse him where making love was concerned. He could whip her up into a sexual frenzy with just a simple look, a touch and a promise of things to come. Time had not dulled her eagerness to fall into his arms.

Finn paused, his arms trembling from the thin control he'd thrown over his rampaging passion. He was raw and open and completely into the moment and when he looked down at Ally—his wife—he saw a flash of something deep behind the arousal shining in her eyes. Was it fear? He had no idea. He didn't want to know because if he did...

She shuttered her eyes closed and drew him down.

He yanked down his jeans and, with a groan, eased into her moist warmth.

Her breath hissed out against his cheek, ending in a gasp as he pushed deeper. Her eyes were still squeezed tight, almost as if it pained her.

"Ally?"

To his amazement, a lone tear leaked out from beneath those smoky lashes and slipped down her cheek. He caught it in a kiss, tasting the hot saltiness before nuzzling her skin.

"Ally? Are you okay? I'm not hurting you?"

Ally groaned, mortified. *You're killing me.* Her heart split in two, the shards stabbing, reopening the old wound. "No. Just keep going."

"You sure? I can—"

"No!" She tightened her legs around his hips, holding him in. "Finish it."

Even though the moment had abruptly shattered, he did as she asked.

It was over too soon. Finally he rolled off and she withdrew, curling up into a ball, her back to him.

They both lay apart, short ragged breaths loud in the cavernous silence. Slowly, the shadows lengthened as the sun disappeared behind gathering storm clouds.

Soon rain began to fall softly. It pattered against the windows, the ocean breeze sweeping a gentle blanket of raindrops inside the open patio door.

She heard Finn get to his feet and draw the door closed.

Then nothing.

In silence she reached for her clothes, pulled on her pants and did up the buttons with an unsteady hand. After the third try she managed to get her shirt over her head.

Glancing over her shoulder, she saw him at the window with his back to her, his glorious body naked and dotted with rain.

She ached to touch him so badly her hands shook.

"That shouldn't have happened," he said gruffly, his back still to her.

Her heart twisted that tiny bit more. He'd hated it. He hadn't wanted her, just what she could give him.

His memory.

"Guess your theory didn't work, huh?"

He turned then, the look on his face unreadable. "I meant I shouldn't have been that rough."

"Oh." She straightened her shirt, feeling lost and incredibly stupid.

"Why were you crying?"

"I wasn't crying."

"Yes, you were."

"I wasn't," she insisted. "I—"

With a soft growl, Finn strode over and grabbed her arms. She gasped, confronted with his ferocious glare.

"Don't lie to me, Ally. I was inside you, this close to your face, and you were crying. Why?"

The look in his eyes wounded a thousand times over,

reached inside and squeezed the very life from her heart. But like the fool she was, she couldn't keep the emotion from bubbling to the surface.

"You make me too vulnerable, Finn! Just like a teenager begging for a scrap of attention. I don't need you to tell me again how I can hardly look after myself, let alone a baby. How I'm not ready, totally selfish and trying to hold on to a dying relationship." Hot irrational anger choked her throat, clogging it until she couldn't think straight. "Yes, running away is something I'm not proud of but I wasn't going to stay with a man who didn't want a pregnant wife!"

Eighteen

Ally's fury crashed to the floor and died a sudden death the very second she realized what she'd said. With a gasp, her hand flew to her mouth but the words hung in the air like a poisoned cloud, floating in to destroy everything in its path.

What have I done?

"Finn. I'm sorry… I didn't mean…" Her words stuttered in her throat, a small cry of distress on her lips.

A car revved up in the street below and screeched around the corner. A breeze sprayed a fine mist of rain against the window and set the wind chime tinkling furiously outside. Yet still the silence was a thousand times more deafening.

"Didn't want…?" Dark frown lines creased his forehead. "I don't understand. I thought I didn't know."

She put a hand to her belly and sighed, swallowing her last shred of resistance. *I'm so sorry, baby. I need to stop fighting this.*

"I had a miscarriage the first time…two weeks after we arrived in Denmark."

"How?"

"It was an accident. I fell down a flight of stairs." She refused to elaborate, knowing no good would come of it. It would serve no purpose to tell him she'd been overwhelmed with anger the first night they'd had that argument, when he'd told her the cold hard truth that Sørensen Silver would always come first.

She'd miscalculated the stairs, her vision blurry with tears.

No one knew. And she would take that secret with her to the grave.

Ally could only stare mutely, her heart twisting at the look of pure pain etched on his face, the profound depth of grief in his eyes. His back straightened as if someone had stuck a knife in it and given a vicious twist.

And to her complete misery, he took a step backward.

Away from her.

"Finn." She swallowed thickly, forging on past his cold, closed expression. How quickly he had turned from passionate lover to less than a complete stranger. "It was…something that just happened."

"Tell me what happened after that."

She dropped her gaze, unable to bear the look in his. "I got out of hospital and we went on with our lives for another two months. But something had changed, something we both knew couldn't be fixed. Then I got a stomach bug. Apparently antibiotics render the pill ineffective."

"In the meantime I told you I didn't want children. Ever."

The underlying bitterness wounded her very soul. Somewhere deep inside, she wept for him—for the confusion, the fury and the desire to lash out that was surely eating away at his control. With a sigh she continued.

"You never talked about your parents' divorce or your

childhood so I guessed there were some issues there that had hurt you," she said quietly. "I didn't realize how much. When we got to Denmark the change in you was astounding. I could see you loved your father and his company, but it's taken me up till now to figure it out. You were afraid your involvement in the business would overshadow everything else in your life—including a child."

"That I'd turn out exactly like my father?" he snapped.

"Yes." She made a move forward, to offer him comfort and understanding but, unsure how he'd take it, stopped herself just in time. "You need to know that I don't blame you for anything."

And incredibly, that was the truth. Dropping her gaze, she gave a sad sigh. Somewhere, somehow, as they had recalled memories and relived their past, she'd purged all bitterness about his decision. Using it as a weapon against someone who couldn't remember didn't change that fact.

Their lovemaking had only compounded it.

The thought was liberating, as if she'd been wearing too-tight shoes that dug and pinched and now she was wiggling her bare toes in the sand.

Finn was still absorbing the shock, a dozen emotions racing over his features. She put her hand on his arm, a soft touch on unyielding stone. He shook it off.

"Why did you agree to help me?" he snarled, green eyes dark and stormy. "After what I did, how could you—"

"How could I not?" she countered. "I could've said no but I didn't. We've been—we are—man and wife. We've shared everything."

A breath hissed out from between his teeth as if she'd insulted him. "What happened after you lost the baby?"

"We argued but always ended up in bed. The last time I told you I was leaving. You offered me money, but I wouldn't take it." She saw him stiffen. "Your father tried to talk me out of leaving, but when he realized I was serious, he drove me to the airport. I came back home to Sydney, found out I was pregnant. So I decided it was best if I just stayed out of your life."

She closed her eyes against the destructive past, the over-whelming abandonment that she'd sworn she'd never go through again, and pushed it from her mind. It was over. She had dealt with it and moved on.

When she opened her eyes, Finn was staring at her, a tense figure of anger and self-loathing.

Her heart ached. "Don't, Finn. Don't do this to yourself. You can't change what happened between us."

"Were you ever planning to tell me this?"

"No."

His features tightened into hard, sharp planes. "Don't you think I deserved to know?"

"And do you feel better knowing?" she asked calmly.

"*For Satan,* Ally! I had a right to know!"

"And now you do." Finally, unable to watch him struggle with this any longer, she went to him. He grabbed her hands, shoved her away.

She tried again.

"Ally. I'm warning you," he growled, imprisoning her wrists.

She twisted free, wrapped her arms around his neck and clung on for dear life. "Just let that anger and regret go. It won't change a thing."

He struggled but determinedly she tightened her grip, pressing herself closer.

Almost immediately heat flared up, scorching through her shirt and into him, reminding her of the intimate connection they still had. His warm breath stuttered, dashing over her neck.

For an eternity they stayed like that, Ally with her arms

around him, Finn straining from her touch, while their bodies were doing something else entirely.

Finally, with a deep, gut-wrenching groan he wrapped his arms tightly around her and gave in.

Ally rested her cheek on his chest, the steady thrum-thrum of his heartbeat a comforting echo of hers. And she could swear it kicked up in tempo while she stood there, absorbing his heat and willing forgiveness into his bones.

"I was a complete fool," Finn muttered against her hair, tentatively stroking the curls. "More than a fool. How on earth you put up with me, I will never know. I wish I could remember."

The sigh she gave ruffled the very edges of his control. He'd wanted so desperately to find fault, something, anything, that would justify leaving Ally after he regained his memory. But now, knowing the full story, he couldn't.

Damn—he couldn't even blame her for walking out on him, for keeping this baby a secret. He'd been a first-class jerk and deserved every inch of her contempt.

She shifted, brought her body more completely up against his. He looked down to see the remnants of an emotional storm settling behind her eyes.

"And I'm sorry," she whispered. "But it's better you can't remember it all. I like this Finn much better." Then she kissed him.

Nineteen

"This is dangerous," Finn muttered against her mouth. "I can't… We shouldn't…"

"I know. But I can't help myself."

His breath hitched.

The desperate desire to blow away the shadows of the man he had been engulfed him. No wonder she didn't want to take anything from him. He'd hurt her so deeply, then had emotionally blackmailed her into helping him.

Yet here she was, her arms wrapped around his neck, forgiving him.

He took his redemption as eagerly as the glorious indulgence of her lips. The softness, the texture was unlike anything he could remember. Her intimate breath on his mouth, the warmth of her hands over his skin.

A thick pounding started in his belly, quickly spreading to his groin. It was like kissing her for the first time all over again. His heart skittered merrily along, caught in the urgency of the moment.

And when he filled himself with her scent his head reeled. It felt like coming home after an eternity in limbo. It was so good. So right.

"Do you want me to keep kissing you, *elskat?*" he murmured, the warm question teasing against her lips.

"Yes."

His mouth trailed molten fire over her jaw and found a sensitive place on her neck, provoking tiny shivers along her skin. He tunneled his fingers into her hair, dragging through the strands with a deep feeling of utmost pleasure.

Something in his chest pinged when she brought passion-darkened gray eyes up to meet his. His skin felt as though someone had set him alight from the inside out, her touch scorching a trail over sensitive flesh while his heart pumped in double-time.

Memories danced and teased just out of his reach and futilely he tried to imprint them before they fled.

Yet even without those memories, this woman who filled his arms so perfectly felt familiar, comfortable. Instinctively he knew what would turn her on. How she liked to be kissed. How her body would shudder and moan and how her spontaneous response would push all his buttons.

When he kissed her again, tenderly, lovingly, then breathed in her musky arousal, he was doomed.

Burning with the need to touch, he bunched her shirt up, then drew his tongue slowly across the tops of swelling creamy breasts cupped by scraps of pink lace.

"So beautiful, *elskat,*" he murmured against the satiny skin, the glorious smell of hot, sweaty woman. Dipping his fingers under the lace, he freed one nipple. Her deep sound of pleasure sent a shot of pure male satisfaction to his groin and in the next instant he took that puckered bud in his mouth, rolling his tongue around it, rasping his teeth against the sensitive flesh.

He gathered her in his arms and took a step backward, until he hit the couch and sat, dragging her across his lap, across his straining erection. Sweat broke out on his brow.

"Ally."

With her name like a groan on his lips, his questing fingers undid her pants, dragged them over her hips and sought the warmth between her legs.

Ally thought she might burst from pleasure. If she pretended really hard, she could imagine his touch possessed the same emotion and intensity like when they were first in love. He caressed, he stroked, he kissed as though the past months and a million regrets had never been.

He brought her to the brink of release with his sinful fingers, a languid, deep stroking rhythm inside her moistened heat so exquisite she almost lost it right then and there.

"Finn…" she pleaded. "Please. I want you inside me."

He paused in his torture, smiling up at her flushed face with a glorious look of wonder. Then slowly, as he kept on with that delicious stroking, she heard the rasp of a zipper.

For one brief second he withdrew, somehow managed to lift her onto his lap and yank down her panties. Then, in one long, slow tease, he slid her down onto his throbbing arousal.

She clenched her teeth and gave a sharp hiss.

Finn stilled. "Does that hurt?"

She shook her head, curls spilling over her shoulders. "It's wonderful." Then she sighed, an erotic sound full of lusty contentment that turned Finn on in a thousand different ways.

He cupped her bottom and set out slowly, rocking her back and forth. Trying to defy the hot explosive need that bubbled in his veins. But when her eyes gazed into his, glazed with passion, it touched something so incredibly pure, so desperate in him that it left his control in the dust.

Her head tipped forward, enveloping them in a fragrant cocoon, the silky hair like feathers teasing his shoulders, his face. Her breath came out in tiny gasps against his cheek. As she bent to capture his lips again and again she moved and rocked above him. He wanted to hold back, wanted her to take pleasure first, to see the glorious satisfaction register in her eyes, but he wasn't sure he could make it. He was just one raw nerve and she was scraping heat over it, taking her with him into the inferno.

A slice of memory speared behind his eyes. Ally, moaning and damp with passion, smelling of blossoms and sex, lying on an unfamiliar bed with her hair spread over the pillow. Him, stripping off her clothes like a man possessed before burying himself in her welcoming core.

A deep and thorough sense of belonging dragged a cry from his lips then sucked away his breath to leave him gasping.

She paused, gently touched his cheek. "What's wrong?" Her voice was threaded with concern.

He shook his head, took her face in his hands and kissed her. "Nothing. Everything is right."

His breath, out of control, blasted across Ally's tender skin, and as he began to move slowly inside her again, his fingers sought and found the tiny bud of arousal that he'd used to reduce her to a quivering heap many times before.

Her mind went blank as her brain shorted out.

She wriggled, strained to escape the sensual torture. "Stop, stop, stop."

"No, *elskat*," he murmured, throwing her off balance by pulling her forward, then conveniently capturing a nipple with his lips. "You can't stop it."

Could someone actually die from pleasure? she thought deliriously as Finn flicked, stroked and kissed her into a frenzy. He was outside and inside, working magic on her body. Her sanity. Her soul.

She felt her release start to build up, sweeping closer like the beginnings of a tidal wave, the pressure swelling inside— hot, wet and furious. She tried to twist, to pull away again, but he evaded her.

"Let me do this. Please." His eyes burned into hers, desire and need and fire alight in the depths.

With a final groan, she lost all control and peaked in a crashing, tumultuous release.

Finn squeezed his eyes shut, desperately clawing for the thin threads of restraint. She was slick and hot, shuddering around him, great aching shudders that pierced his self-control and tugged mercilessly.

He couldn't hold on anymore.

Ally watched the release flood his face, emotion shoot across every feature and tighten the muscles. A low groan, almost primal in its depths, feathered across her neck.

With Finn buried deep inside her, she ran her hands down his sweat-soaked arms, feeling every dip and bulge of his body, tempered steel beneath hot, satin-smooth skin. When he reached for her, she let him draw her down into his embrace.

Don't fool yourself. Remember this isn't forever.

Twenty

The sun slowly set, defiantly shining through the heavy bedroom curtains.

Ally stirred next to him, her hair trapped under his arm, one silky leg thrown over his. He swept his gaze over her face—the freckles he'd lazily kissed again and again, those long sooty lashes that had fluttered closed with an earthy sigh then flown open when his tongue had teased her back to the brink of climax. That wonderful mouth that had laughed and sighed and done its fair share of teasing his flesh.

Flesh that suddenly hardened at that thought.

Gently, so as not to wake her, Finn placed his palm against her belly, slowly testing the slight swell beneath.

His baby.

Emotion ripped at his chest, winding him.

He had hurt Ally so much, the selfish demanding man he'd been. Yet miraculously, he'd been given a chance to put it right.

And now he was here. Ally was in his bed. And they were still married.

"Can you feel that?" she murmured.

Her sleepy gray eyes were open as her hand tentatively covered his, still on her naked belly. A tiny fluttering erupted under his palm. Wonderingly, he stroked her skin.

"It's the first time I felt him move," she whispered, her face reflecting the awe he felt.

He swooped down for her mouth, wanting her fierce response to match his and assuage the tainted memories of his past that he'd branded her with. But Ally wouldn't let him. Instead she melted into him, into the kiss, with such aching tenderness that he groaned in frustration. *Damn her for understanding. Damn her for forgiving me.*

And damn me for loving her.

It was almost as if it were their first time all over again, Ally thought dreamily as he moved to cover her body with kisses. His mouth, so harsh and demanding, had softened into a kind of divinity that made her want to sink right into his skin and stay there forever. He stroked her hair, gently arranging it over her shoulders so her nipples poked though the strands. He paid loving tribute to them, sucking, rolling and nipping, sending glorious warmth pounding through her skin. Her groin began to throb in anticipation, her fingers searching for his silken heat that pressed urgently against her thigh. This time he let her take him, let her guide him into her hot wetness. And when he slid inside, she gave a blissful cry of triumph, her head thrown back.

"Look, *elskat*. Look at us."

She followed his gaze to the full-length mirror across the room, to her eyes wide and shocked. The bed sheets lay tangled and forgotten on the floor, displaying their entwined limbs to stark perfection. Her legs wrapped around his waist and locked at the ankles. His dark-brown arms cradled her body; long, elegant fingers splayed over her breasts.

As she stared, his gaze met hers in their reflection and his mouth dipped, took one erect nipple in his mouth and sucked.

She made a mewling sound that sounded like a plea.

"Watch us, Ally," he commanded as her eyes began to close.

So she did. She remained transfixed as his hand slipped between their sweaty bodies and found the very core of her hot, slick heat. With confident authority his fingers massaged her and through the glorious burst of exploding pleasure she thought she heard his breath falter, felt his arms tremble.

With green eyes locked on nearly-black in the mirror, he began to whip her up into such a passion that she thought she'd go over the brink. His lips went back to hers, tasting, teasing, arousing. His hands cupped one breast while the other weaved magic on her most sensitive spot. And his hot breath feathered across her skin, scorched her to the point of combustion.

When she cried out and began to shudder, Finn threw her leg over his shoulder and thrust deep into her welcoming body.

Jeg elsker dig.

I love you.

Finn knew better than to say those words aloud. Knew better than to tell her what she didn't want to hear. So he showed her instead, with every deep kiss, with every tender touch. With every strong stroke he rocked into her damp enfolding heat, Finn loved her.

And if he couldn't change the past then he would make damn sure their future began right.

Which meant telling her the truth.

Half an hour later, Finn said quietly, "I have something to tell you."

"Hmm?"

She was lying in his arms, a hand gently stroking his chest.

"There's more to—" He ended on a curse as the sharp trill of his cell phone on the dresser interrupted his admission.

When he hesitated, Ally sat up. "Answer it," She released the sheet and reached for her robe, easing her arms into the sleeves. "It could be important."

Finn stared at her, at the profile of soft cheek and stubborn jawline, at the tumble of curls sweeping over her shoulders. The elegant, erotic dip and curve of her naked back and the remembered memory of touching and stroking every inch of that velvety skin.

Without looking back, she said quietly again, "It could be important," before slipping out the door.

Unable to refute her statement, Finn picked up the phone. "What?"

"Finn?"

He rubbed his temple, recognizing the voice of his cousin, Louisa. *"Ja?"*

"Check your e-mails. I've got something you'll want to see."

He walked out of the bedroom and into cavernous silence. "Ally?"

As his heart began to pick up tempo, he strode into the kitchen. On the table sat a note in her familiar loopy handwriting.

"Gone to get breakfast. Back soon. A. X"

With a sigh he turned back to the lounge, to his laptop on the coffee table.

Seconds dragged as he watched it boot up then go through the motions of receiving e-mail, time recorded with every sharp tick on the hallway clock.

Then it was there.

The final answer.

The end to his quest. The end to him and Ally.

No.

He took a gulp of air and began to read.

Louisa had had the foresight to scan the letter—dated the day of the accident—and e-mail it to him. He read it once, then again, disbelieving.

Dear Finn,

This letter and hand-written codicil is serving as a stopgap just in case something happens. And if you're reading this, it means something *has* and I didn't have a chance to formalize it and talk to you.

As you know, I'm a man of action, not words. But please accept my apology if you felt that you'd missed out on me being there for you. That is my one biggest regret but, of course, being my son, you never let on.

I did the best I knew how, and that meant providing a stable home after your mother died, keeping you fed, in clothes and giving you a top-notch education. I even thought that by marrying Marlene I could somehow give you another mother figure, even though at seven you were such a grown-up little man already.

Still, we know how that turned out and I'm sorry.

Which brings me to this letter. The doctors are going to give me a good going over and I don't expect anything unforeseen, but you know I've always planned for any eventuality. I will be amending my will anyway but this codicil will now serve my final wishes."

Finn blinked and paused, then drew in a ragged breath, once then twice. Then he continued.

Forty-five percent of all Sørensen Silver's shares are to go to you, with the remaining forty-five shared amongst the current board members, Louisa included. Ally will receive a ten percent share. You know that Louisa has been an integral part of the designing team for years, so that would hardly be a shock. But Ally?

I liked her from the moment we met. I started to love her like a daughter. Thanks to her, I began to realize something. Family is more important than working fifteen-hour days. There's no time like now to get to know my son, to live and experience life outside the boardroom. She was my wake-up call, if you like. She was good for you and you...well, you just couldn't see that. Too stubborn, too focused on work.

Sounds like someone we know, hmm?

Okay, now I'm rambling and you know how I hate that. I contemplated a reconciliation demand but that would've tied the company up for years in court. The next best thing is this controlling share which will keep her in your life, force you to talk to her.

Because I did so little of it, I strongly recommend communication. Work it out. In the end, I know you still love her and that's all that matters.

Your father,
Nikolai Sørensen.

Finn sat back on the chair and drew in a staggering breath, his brain overwhelmed with discovery.

He'd thought he'd understood the kind of man his father was. Distant and driven. In control. Focused. He'd accepted that from an early age, had even come to admire the way Nikolai had operated in the business world. So he'd mirrored those traits and had quickly become known for his sharp decisions, his tireless pursuit of excellence.

But now…

The rug had been firmly pulled out from under his feet, leaving him confused and unsure.

He strangled out a short laugh. It wasn't exactly how his father had planned it, but thanks to the man's actions, he'd still managed the correct end result.

A key rattled in the lock and Ally stepped through the door. Her hair was ruffled into a seductive mess, her skin flushed. Finn took a moment to take his fill of her, the unbelievable sight of this amazing woman. His gaze dipped to the non-existent curve of her belly below her white T-shirt.

The mother of his child. The one person who had literally changed his world.

You can stop searching.

His heart began to beat just that little bit faster.

"Croissants were a ten-minute wait. I thought we could go to…" She paused at the look on his face, gently closed the door behind her. "What's the matter?"

He took a deep steadying breath, trying to center himself. "I know what happened."

He waited a heartbeat, then another. The quicksilver play of emotions flitted across her face, widening then narrowing her eyes with shock…elation.…

Pain.

"Your memory's back?" Her tiny breathy voice was part joy, part hurt as she carefully placed the keys on the hall stand.

"No. Louisa called me. The codicil's been found."

Panic surged through Ally's body as her entire world tipped up and she fell off the edge.

There is no happily ever after for you and Finn. Did you forget?

"So. Okay. Good. You found the codicil." She crossed her arms, trying to stop the trembling that had started in her legs and was now spreading quickly to her belly. "Where was it?"

Looking weary and drained, he dragged a hand across his stubbled jaw. "Nikolai wrote it at the hospital and got a nurse to witness it. When he was in surgery, Marlene bribed the nurse to steal it. Apparently the woman thought she could make more as a criminal and tried to blackmail her."

"How did you find all this out?"

He shook his head disbelievingly. "The thief's husband came to us. He found the papers and contacted the company." He hesitated for a second, then two, as if unsure how to proceed.

"So. Okay." Ally swallowed the pain welling up in her throat. *Don't you cry. Don't you dare cry.* "That means you'll be going back home. Did you get the deed for this place drawn up? I'll also need you to sign those divorce papers—"

If she'd just slapped him across the face he couldn't look more shocked. "Ally—"

"Don't make this harder than it has to be, Finn," she said firmly, belying the devastation in her heart. "You need to go." *What about what I need?* "And the company needs you. You *are* Sørensen Silver now."

"And so are you."

"No, I'm not."

"My father gave you a ten-percent controlling share."

She took a step backward and bumped into the couch, eyes wide. "What?"

"That's what I was about to tell you before. I have forty-five percent, the rest of the board has the same. You got ten."

The tingle of panic shot through her veins. "Why would Nikolai do that?"

"Because he loved you like a daughter."

Choking back sudden tears, she said in a small voice, "I don't want it."

"You've got it."

"I don't care. I'll…" She groped, desperate for a solution. "I'll sell it back to you." She tunneled her hands into her hair, then stilled as a horrible thought suddenly occurred. "How long have you known?"

His silence, the look in his eyes, said it all.

She blinked incredulously. "You knew. All the time you *knew!*"

"*Ja.*"

The pain was like a physical wound, ripping her chest apart. "You promised me. No lies." A new thought twisted inside, burning a hole in her gut. "Was this part of your plan? To keep me in the dark so I'd have no choice but to turn to you?"

"*No!*" His furious denial shocked her so much she blinked. He went on more calmly, "I don't want any more secrets between us. And even if we hadn't found the codicil, I'm still going to look after you and the baby. I—"

"I don't need to be looked after." *I want you!* Ally fought with the sob in her throat, choked down the tears. "Max offered me my old job back. I can support myself. And I don't want a part of something that tore us apart. I never wanted it."

He gave her a look that said she was being unreasonable or hysterical or both. "Do you think I'd walk away and leave my wife and child to fend for themselves?"

No! It was worse than she'd imagined. Instead of him leaving—one big rip of the Band-Aid—Finn was coming back to do this all over again. And after a while, a year, maybe two, he'd get the yearning for his homeland, become bored with not being on the company frontline and leave. Again. She'd be forced onto that damned roller-coaster ride, the highs of his return, the uncertainties of his extended absences. They would dredge up the same arguments and she would feel exactly the same, loving him so desperately she'd do anything to have him.

Even entertaining the thought of staying married.

She loved him desperately. So desperately she'd willingly renege on all those promises she'd made, all those vows not to have her heart broken again and never, ever to leave herself so vulnerable.

Ally's insides clenched. Hadn't he taken enough? What more could she possibly give without losing her very sanity?

"Do it for our child, Ally. Take my offer," he said softly.

She firmly swallowed the tears that threatened to spill over. It was an offer. Not a declaration of love, not a commitment. An offer. Just like another of his business deals.

She shook her head miserably and turned away, unable to stand the perfect, painful sight of him any longer. "No."

She heard him sigh. "Ally."

"Please, just go, Finn. You found the codicil so there's no reason for you to stay."

And because she couldn't bear the pain anymore, she pushed past him, ran into the bedroom and locked the door.

He pounded and yelled but, with a whimper, she curled up into a ball on the bed and shoved her hands over her ears.

The slam of the front door a few minutes later confirmed his departure. With a moan of despair, she began to sob.

Ally watched a passing plane fly by the bedroom window and knew that it was finally over. Surprisingly, she didn't cry again—not when she opened the door, not when she sat on the couch, staring at the carefully folded sheaf of papers on the coffee table, numb with shock.

Maybe I've finally gone insane, she thought dispassionately.

Why else would she let fear of the past still continue to keep a stranglehold on her actions?

He wanted to meet his responsibilities and support the baby. That was a lot more than other men offered and she would be an idiot to pass up that chance.

But the cold, hard truth was that Finn wasn't in love with her. She shouldn't have been surprised about his offer to support the baby: duty and honor always came first with him. But duty was not enough. She wanted more. And as much as she wanted him, it killed her to know he would never turn his back on everything just to be with her.

Which meant she had no part in it.

She scowled at the patio doors, at the now-annoying wind chime tinkling merrily in the breeze. Now that she owned a controlling share of Sørensen Silver, Finn was under no financial obligation to help her. She could live comfortably on the profits or sell her shares back to him. He could walk away without looking back.

Which is exactly what he did.

So now that she had what she wanted, why was she so damn miserable?

The baby. Think of the baby.

Yet all she could think of was the missed chances, all the hours they'd spent together when she'd thought of confessing her feelings, reasoning be damned.

And now it was too late. She had the papers to prove it.

She reached out for the bundle and wearily unfolded it. He'd left his end of the bargain and signed her—

Frowning, she flicked through the pages, searching for the divorce decree and the ownership papers. Instead it was just a bunch of e-mails from that darn memory box.

What on earth…?

She slapped them down on the table and sprang to her

feet. Finn had left and broken his promise. She had no home. They were still married. Her life was exactly back to where she'd been a month ago, except now she was haunted by the bittersweet memories of his passion and betrayal.

The snick of a key in the lock made her glance up and suddenly he stood there framed in the door, looking like every dream she'd ever had, every desire unfulfilled.

"Dammit, Finn, what the hell are you playing at?"

Dreams didn't scowl at her like that. Nor did they slam doors and glare right back.

"You'll have to be more specific." He tossed a bakery bag on the table. The smell of warm flaky pastry floated into her nostrils, confusing her.

"I thought you'd left!"

"Why on earth would I do that?"

"You found the codicil—"

He took a deep breath then let it out in a groan of frustration. "Forget about the stupid codicil for one second! I'm in love with you! Why would I want to leave?"

She blinked. "You what?"

Then something strange happened. All that bluster drained from his face, leaving him looking suddenly vulnerable.

"Why did you—?"

"What made you—?"

They both paused, until Finn closed the space between them and put a silencing finger on her lips. "Let me speak."

He rubbed his palm over his chin, taking a few seconds to gather his thoughts and looking so wonderfully touchable and yet so untouched that it made Ally want to weep.

"I don't want to leave," he finally said. "Not again. I can't do it. *For helve,* Ally…" He took a shuddering breath, the look in his eyes deadly serious, "Do you know you just scare the hell out of me?"

Her lip started to tremble. "Why?"

"Because I had you once but threw you away. And knowing that absolutely kills me. Because you know me inside out, as no one else does. You understand me. Because—" he hesitated, as if trying to steady the waver in his voice "—I look at you and my...my heart just stops. I want you. I love you."

Shock sent her back into the rigid coffee table as she shook her head in denial.

"Believe me, *elskat,* I certainly didn't count on it."

He looked so downright aggravated that she stuffed back the hysterical laugh welling up inside. But before she could say anything, he produced some papers from his back pocket. "I took so long because I went to sign these."

"The apartment?" She took the sheaf from him, unrolled it. Two shiny keys fell out.

"No. A house. Up on Beach Road. Six bedrooms, ocean views, balcony, huge backyard."

"You can't..."

"I can. Paid cash. It's ours."

She blurted out the first thing that came to mind. "What are we going to do with six bedrooms?"

He grinned. "More kids?"

She put out a trembling hand to cover her mouth. "I mean—" she swallowed "—you can't do this again. What if you remember? What if everything we've shared these past weeks is too good to be true? I couldn't stand it if you ended up hating me all over again." She searched his face, begging him to understand.

Finn saw the raw hurt, the panic shadowing her eyes and fell just that little more in love. He'd put her through so much pain, so much heartache. He'd made her doubt herself, doubt the sincerity of his actions.

The loathing he felt for the man he'd once been engulfed him for agonizing heartbeats, until he knew what he had to do. He had to show her how much he loved her so she'd never doubt him again. Ever.

"Ally, I wish I could tell you why I did all those things before, but I will never completely understand it," he said softly, resting his hands on her shoulders and staring into her wide vulnerable eyes. "Yes they happened and I am sorry for that. Yes, I kept quiet about your share of the company because I wasn't sure we would find the codicil. I couldn't get your hopes up just to destroy them. You have to believe me." He was surprised to hear his voice break, feel his hands shake.

She said nothing, just dropped her chin and let the curtain of hair fall across her face. Gently, almost reverently, he tucked it back behind her ear.

"The man you once knew is gone. And if you let me, I'll spend the rest of our lives showing you. Ally, *elskat,* look at me."

She brought those eyes up to meet his, turbulent and threaded with worry. "I might never get all my memory back. But what I do know is enough. Your smile, the way your hair slides across your face. The way you smell. And the way I loved you. The way I love you now," he amended, his throat thick with emotion. "A love of respect and honesty and hope. I've been given a second chance with you. To be a family. I want that so much," he laid a hand over her belly, thinking of the life that grew within, of the second chance he'd been handed like a gift from heaven. "I want this baby and I want you. My wife."

The wife he'd never known. And for that he would be completely and utterly grateful. Out of tragedy came a blessing he would never cease to marvel at. It blew him away at the very thought.

"I remember…" He took a shuddering breath under her unblinking gaze. "I remember it rained the day we met—your shirt was see-through and you were wearing a red bra. I remember our wedding day, the way you couldn't stop giggling at the celebrant. And I remember feeling nothing but a deep, aching loss when you left me, as though someone had severed a part of my soul. But most of all—" he swept his eyes over her face, coming to rest on her trembling mouth "—I remember I loved you. I still do. Which is why I'm staying here. With you."

She shook her head disbelievingly. "What about the company? Your family? Friends?"

"How can I explain?" His sigh shuddered through him as he grasped for the words. "That life was killing me. You could see it, even tried to convince me. It's taken the accident to show me what was really going on—how I need you. I don't want to go back if it means losing you. The lawyers can sort out this codicil mess and the company…" He blew out a breath. "Nikolai had been negotiating an expansion into the Asia Pacific market. Sydney was his first choice and if you're willing, I'm going to head the team."

"But—"

"I know what you're thinking." He put his hands on her arms, stroked down the length. "But this time it will be different. Work won't come between us again. I'll hire extra people, whatever it takes. If I *want* to work, that is. Being full-time parents has a certain appeal." He gave her an uncertain smile.

"You not work? I must be delirious."

Tentative threads of hope began to weave around his heart, only faltering when she shook her head and said weakly, "You can't give up everything for me…"

"I wouldn't. You, this baby, our future—that's my everything. Before you I was just a bitter, selfish man."

"No. You were just driven. Focused. I admired that. I still do."

He shook his head. "Defending me again. I must have been a fool to let you go."

"At last, something we do agree on."

At that precise moment, when she smiled, nothing in his life compared to the relief flooding his heart. He pulled her into his arms and welcomed her warm heat like a man who'd been left in the cold for way too long. "We both made mistakes. And my biggest one—" he rested his forehead against hers, took a shuddering breath "—is that I let you go. I won't let that happen again, *elskede*."

My love. Ally closed her eyes as tears began to well up.

"For someone not prone to flowery speeches, that was a doozy."

She felt his smile stretch across her cheek and her heart swelled up, threatening to choke off her air. He was everything she was still so deathly scared of, yet everything she dared hope for.

So she went with the only option her heart would allow— with one deep breath she leaped over the cliff edge.

"Okay," she whispered, slowly opening her eyes. "You've got me. Only because you never *didn't* have me. I've never stopped loving you, Finn. These past weeks only proved that. I know you've changed. I saw it every day. I just didn't want to believe until now."

He reached out and gently swiped away the track of tears from her cheek.

"I always seem to be crying around you." She gave a watery laugh.

With her heart thumping like a winter thunderstorm, his lips came down to softly tease hers. "Sad, *lille skat?*"

"No. It's these damned hormones."

He chuckled. "It's not me?"

"It's you, Finn. It's always been you."

Then she kissed him—deeply, thoroughly, with all the longing and desperation of the past months spent apart and alone. She kissed him, knowing beyond a doubt this time that they were absolutely made for each other.

"I have a few conditions," she finally said after a long moment.

"Yes?"

"That we won't let an argument come between us again."

"Done."

"And that work stays at work. Weekends, evenings are ours."

"Of course. That it?"

She nodded and his arms tightened, hands sweeping up her back and into her hair. "Now say you love me again," he murmured against her mouth.

As his palms cupped her face she linked her fingers in his, heat covering heat. *"Jeg elsker dig."*

He kissed her cheeks with such incredible tenderness that she thought her heart would explode right out through her ribcage with joy.

Her Danish Viking. Her heart soared for the glorious future ahead of them, blood pounding so hard she could hear it reverberating in her head.

His hand swept down to her stomach, to the tiny life that was growing inside her, and his eyes reflected such love, such elation, that her whole body ached just to look at him.

"And I love you, Alexandra McKnight," he said softly, the curve of his smile against her lips. "Be prepared to hear it often."

Epilogue

Nikolai Jakob Sørensen screamed his way into the world, arms flailing and fists clenched in glorious newborn anger.

Ally dragged her gaze away from the wonder of her perfect, pink, scrunched-up son to her husband, his face flushed with bursting pride, fingers touching Nikolai's tiny hands in gentle wonderment.

At the sight of his large, strong hand stroking her son's fragile one, her chest swelled with so much love that her breath hitched thickly in her throat. The emotion on Finn's face twisted his features into something so wondrous that she thought she'd burst into tears right then and there.

Then he met her gaze and smiled. In that smile she saw such love, such happiness, that she felt completely and utterly content.

"Your mother and grandma are waiting outside," the midwife interrupted gently. "Shall I let them in?"

"Not yet," Ally answered, her damp eyes still on her husband. "I just want to enjoy the moment a bit longer."

"Happy, *lille skat?*" Finn tucked a damp curl behind her ear.

"Perfect. I have a baby, a beautiful home, a shiny two-book contract, a syndicated column and a successful, gorgeous husband with a flourishing jewelry business. What more could I want?"

"I'm *after* the book contract?" he teased.

Her answering laugh was cut short when their lips met over their baby's head to seal the perfect moment with a perfect kiss.

* * * * *

Silhouette Desire

There was only one man for the job—
an impossible-to-resist maverick
she knew she didn't dare fall for.

MAVERICK
(#1827)

BY *NEW YORK TIMES*
BESTSELLING AUTHOR
JOAN HOHL

"Will You Do It for One Million Dollars?"

Any other time, Tanner Wolfe would have balked at being
hired by a woman. Yet Brianna Stewart was desperate to
engage the infamous bounty hunter. The price was just
high enough to gain Tanner's interest…Brianna's beauty
definitely strong enough to keep it. But he wasn't about
to allow her to tag along on his mission. He worked
alone. Always had. Always would. However, he'd never
confronted a more determined client than Brianna. She
wasn't taking no for an answer—not about anything.

Perhaps a million-dollar bounty was not the only thing
this maverick was about to gain….

Look for MAVERICK

Available October 2007 wherever you buy books.

Ria Sterling has the gift—or is it a curse?—
of seeing a person's future in his or her
photograph. Unfortunately, when detective
Carrick Jones brings her a missing person's
case, she glimpses his partner's ID—and
sees imminent murder. And when her vision
comes true, Ria becomes the prime suspect.
Carrick isn't convinced this beautiful woman
committed the crime…but does he believe
she has the special powers to solve it?

Look for

Seeing Is Believing

by

Kate Austin

Available October
wherever you buy books.

® HARLEQUIN®

Mediterranean NIGHTS™

Sail aboard the luxurious Alexandra's Dream and experience glamour, romance, mystery and revenge!

Coming in October 2007...

AN AFFAIR TO REMEMBER

by

Karen Kendall

When Captain Nikolas Pappas first fell in love with Helena Stamos, he was a penniless deckhand and she was the daughter of a shipping magnate. But he's never forgiven himself for the way he left her—and fifteen years later, he's determined to win her back.

Though the attraction is still there, Helena is hesitant to get involved. Nick left her once...what's to stop him from doing it again?